Noodlehead Nightmares

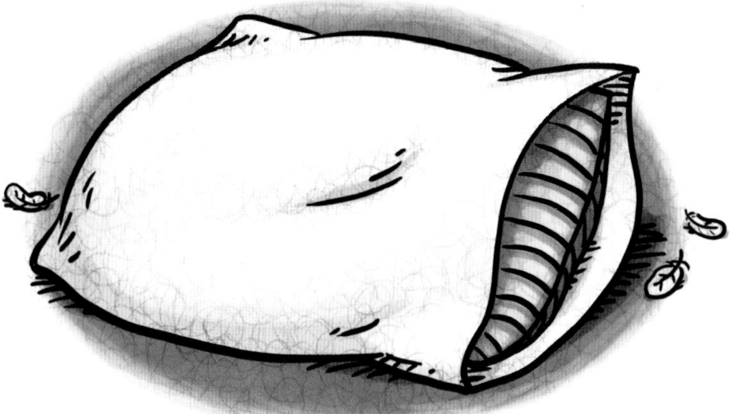

by Tedd Arnold
Martha Hamilton
and Mitch Weiss

illustrated by Tedd Arnold

Holiday House / New York

For Bobbie and Keith—T. A.

In memory of Jeff, whose funny IQ was off the charts—M. H. and M. W.

Authors' Notes—Story Sources for *Noodlehead Nightmares*

The motifs to which we refer in the information that follows are from *The Storyteller's Sourcebook: A Subject, Title, and Motif Index to Folklore Collections for Children* by Margaret Read MacDonald, 1st edition, (Detroit: Gale, 1982) and 2nd edition (Detroit: Gale, 2001). Several references are also made to *The Book of Noodles: Stories of Simpletons; or, Fools and Their Follies*, a scholarly work by W.A. Clouston (London: Eliot Stock Publishers, 1888).

What a Nightmare!

The theme of fools not being able to find their own legs is a common one in world folktales. The motif for this story is: *J2021 Numskulls cannot find their own legs.* W.A. Clouston describes Icelandic and Scottish variations on pp. 32-33 of *The Book of Noodles*. Variations of the story written for children can be found in: "The Men with Mixed-Up Feet," in *Noodlehead Stories: World Tales Kids Can Read and Tell* by Martha Hamilton and Mitch Weiss (Atlanta: August House Publishers, 2000)/"The Mixed-Up Feet and the Silly Bridegroom," in *Zlateh the Goat and Other Stories* by Isaac Bashevis Singer (New York: Harper & Row, 1966)/"How the Twelve Clever Brothers Got Their Feet Mixed Up," in *The Twelve Clever Brothers and Other Fools: Folktales from Russia* by Mirra Ginsburg (NY: J.B. Lippincott, 1979).

The Best Dream

The theme of two characters arguing over food and a trickster settling the fight by dividing it for them, all the while really eating it, is told around the world. We found variations from both Africa and Japan where two cats fight over a piece of cheese and a monkey settles the argument. In a version from Hungary, two bears find a piece of cheese and are tricked by a fox. The motif is: *K452 Unjust umpire misappropriates disputed goods.* Interesting variations include:"Dividing the Cheese," in *Catlore: Tales from Around the World* retold by Marjorie Zaum (NY: Atheneum, 1985)/"Dog, Cat, and Monkey," in *The Oxfam Book of Children's Stories: South & North, East & West* edited by Michael Rosen (Cambridge, MA: Candlewick Press, 1992)/ "The Two Foolish Cats" in *The Sea of Gold: And Other Tales from Japan* adapted by Yoshiko Uchida (NY: Scribner's, 1965)/*Two Greedy Bears: Adapted from a Hungarian Folktale* by Mirra Ginsburg (NY: Macmillan, 1976).

Another common theme found in this story is settling an argument over food by agreeing that whoever has the best dream will get to eat the food *(motif: K444 Dream bread: the most wonderful dream).* One character always eats it while everyone else is asleep. In a Navajo story, Coyote, Skunk and Porcupine find a piece of meat and finally agree that whoever has the most beautiful dream will get to eat it all by himself. That is exactly what Porcupine does while the others are napping. Variations can be found in: "The Beautiful Dream," in *Stories in My Pocket: Tales Kids Can Tell* by Martha Hamilton and Mitch Weiss (Golden, CO: Fulcrum Publishing, 1996)/"Three Dreams," in *Noodles, Nitwits, and Numskulls* by Maria Leach (New York: Scholastic, 1961).

Bedtime for Noodleheads

The inspiration for this story came from two tiny noodle tales from ancient Greece described by W.A. Clouston in *The Book of Noodles*. In one story, a man dreams that he got a nail in his foot and decides that he should never sleep barefoot again (p. 6) (motif: *F1068.5 Fool dreams he hurt foot*). In the other, a fool uses a jar as a pillow after putting feathers inside because he thinks the feathers would make the jar soft (pp. 5-6). A similar story from Ireland, "The Fool's Feather Pillow," can be found in *Noodlehead Stories: World Tales Kids Can Read and Tell* by Martha Hamilton and Mitch Weiss (Atlanta: August House Publishers, 2000).

Text copyright © 2016 by Tedd Arnold, Martha Hamilton and Mitch Weiss
Illustrations copyright © 2016 by Tedd Arnold
All Rights Reserved
HOLIDAY HOUSE is registered in the U.S. Patent and Trademark Office.
Printed and Bound in November 2015 at Toppan Leefung Printing Co., Ltd., DongGuan City, China.
The artwork was rendered digitally using Photoshop software.
www.holidayhouse.com
First Edition
1 3 5 7 9 10 8 6 4 2
Library of Congress Cataloging-in-Publication Data

Arnold, Tedd, author, illustrator.
[Short stories. Selections]
Noodlehead nightmares / by Tedd Arnold, Martha Hamilton and Mitch Weiss ; illustrated by Tedd Arnold.
— First edition.
pages cm
Summary: Brothers Mac and Mac star in this collection of bedtime tales inspired by folktales about fools
from around the world.
ISBN 978-0-8234-3566-1 (hardcover)
[1. Fools and jesters—Fiction. 2. Bedtime—Fiction. 3. Brothers—Fiction. 4. Humorous stories.]
I. Hamilton, Martha, author. II. Weiss, Mitch, 1951- author. III. Title.
PZ7.A7379Ns 2016
[E]—dc23
2015022726

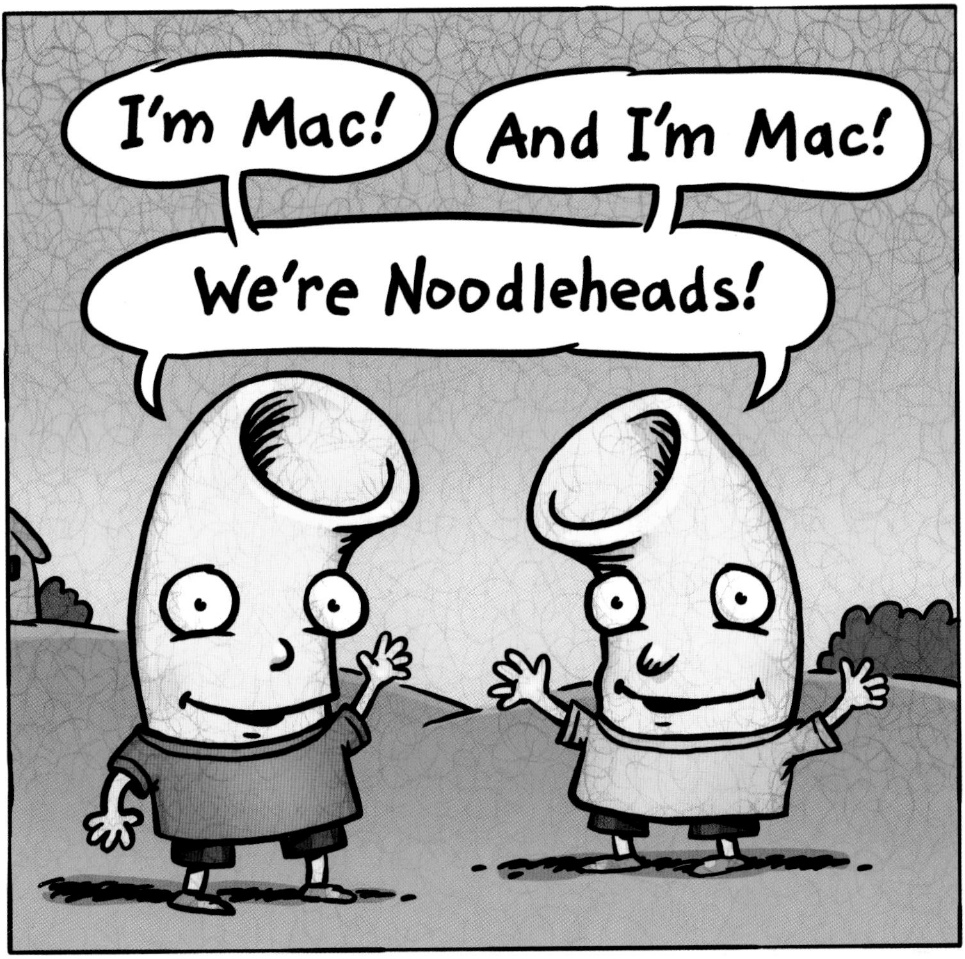
I'm Mac!
And I'm Mac!
We're Noodleheads!

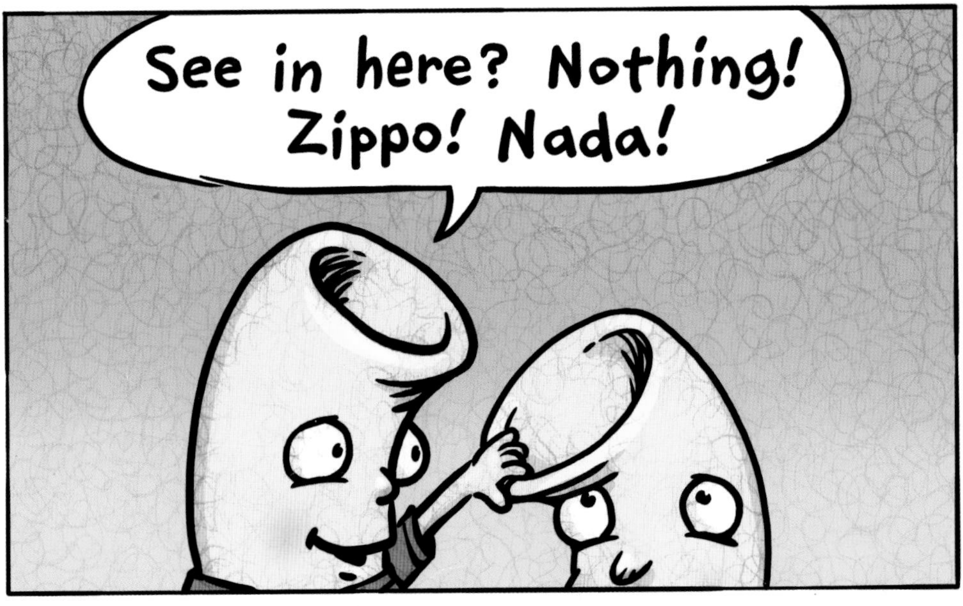
See in here? Nothing!
Zippo! Nada!

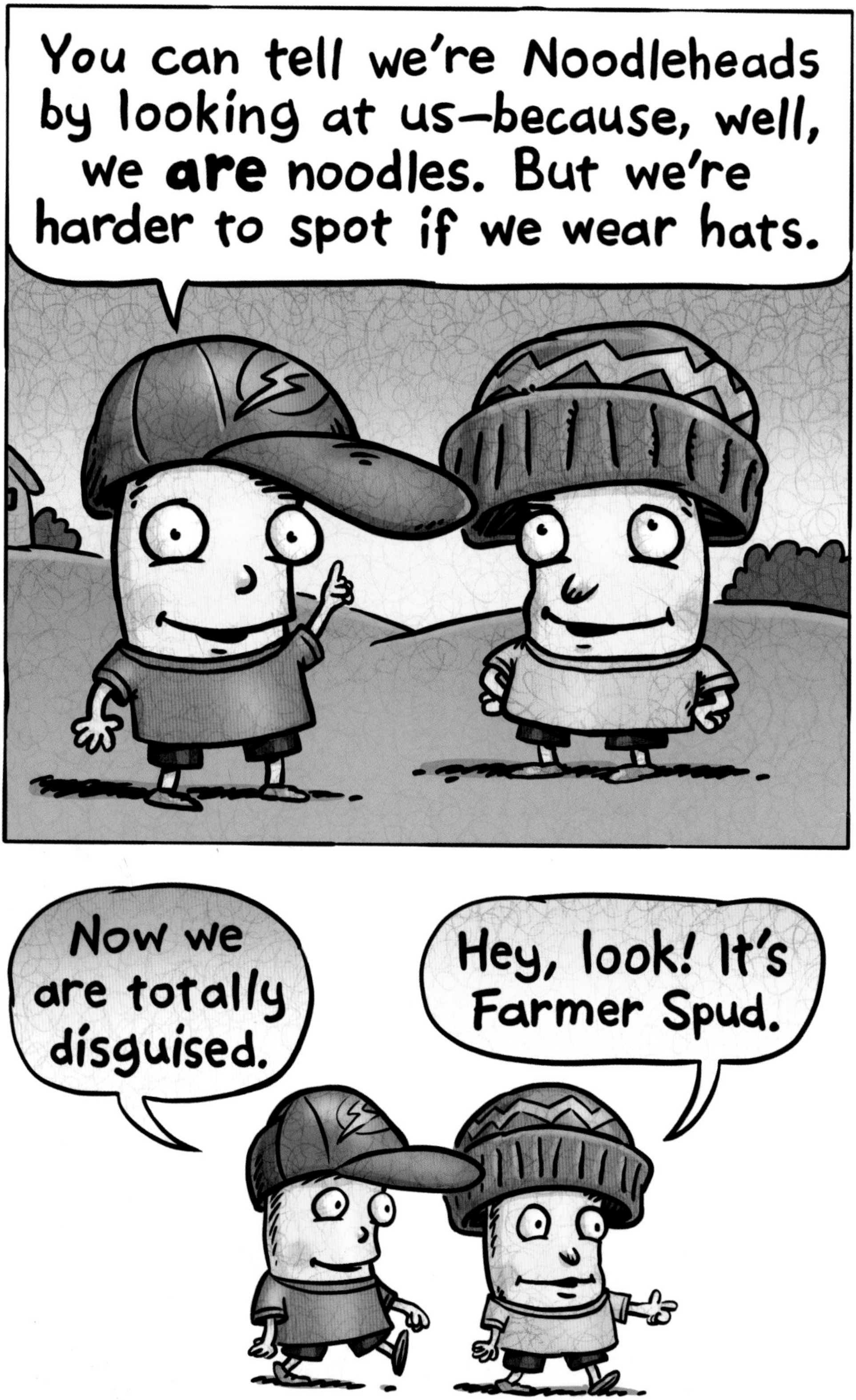
You can tell we're Noodleheads by looking at us—because, well, we **are** noodles. But we're harder to spot if we wear hats.
Now we are totally disguised.
Hey, look! It's Farmer Spud.

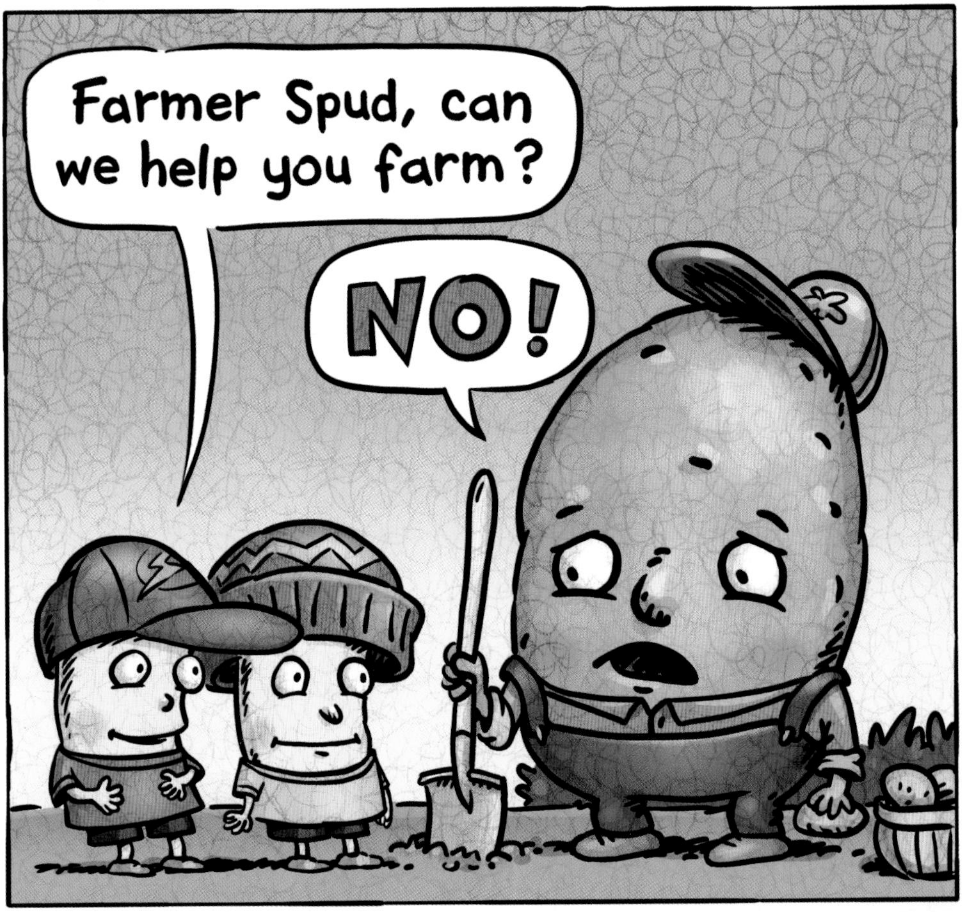
Farmer Spud, can we help you farm?
NO!

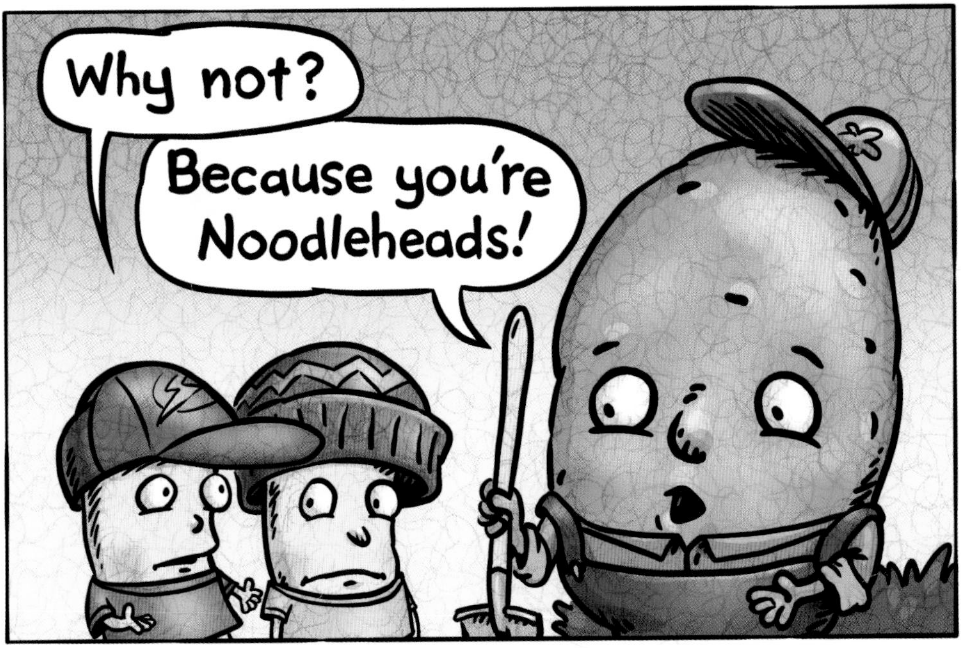
Why not?
Because you're Noodleheads!

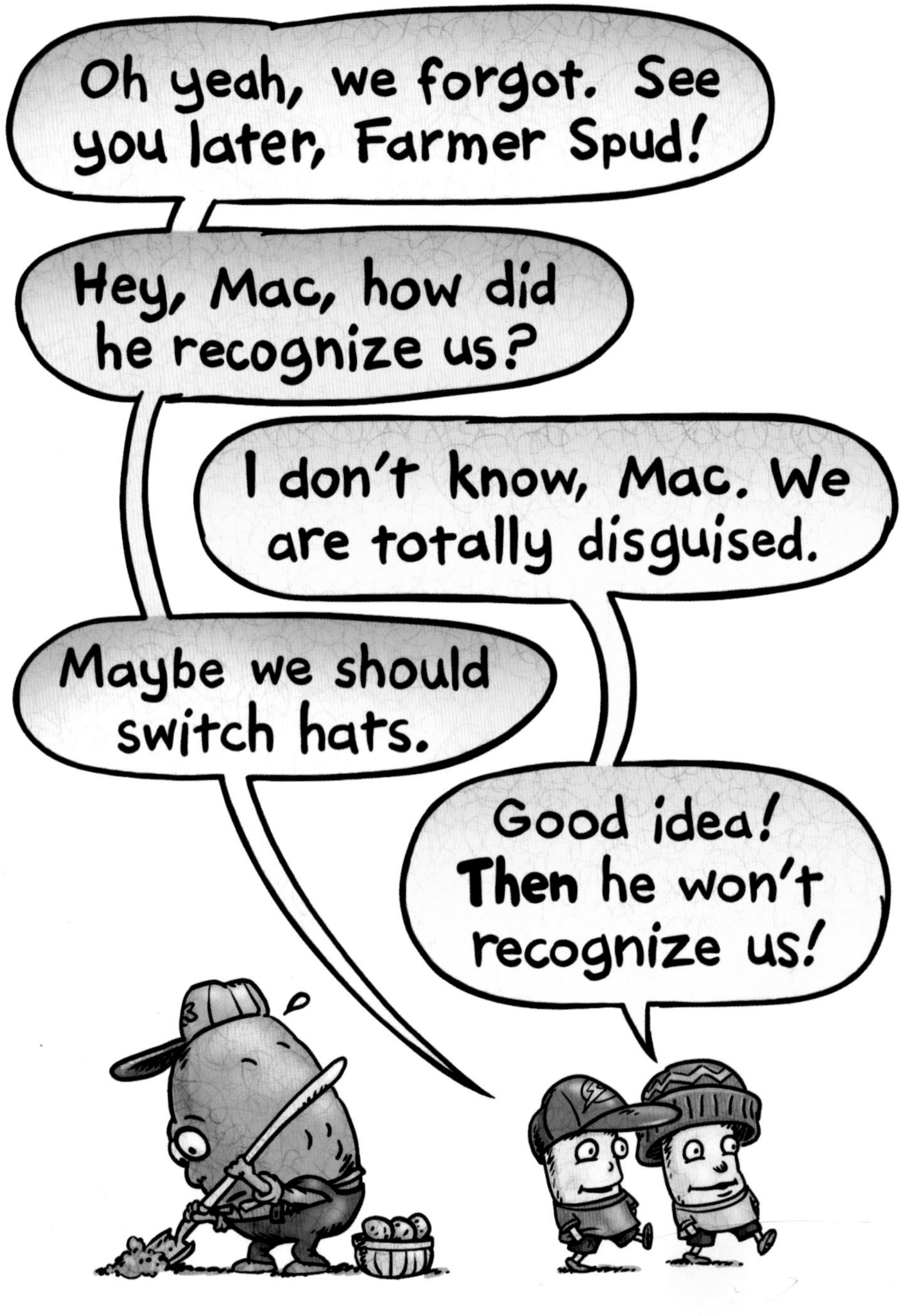
Oh yeah, we forgot. See you later, Farmer Spud!
Hey, Mac, how did he recognize us?
I don't know, Mac. We are totally disguised.
Maybe we should switch hats.
Good idea! **Then** he won't recognize us!

NOODLEHEAD NIGHTMARES

CHAPTER 1

WHAT A NIGHTMARE!

One night, Mac and Mac made an announcement to their mother.

From now on, we are sleeping outside.

And why is that?

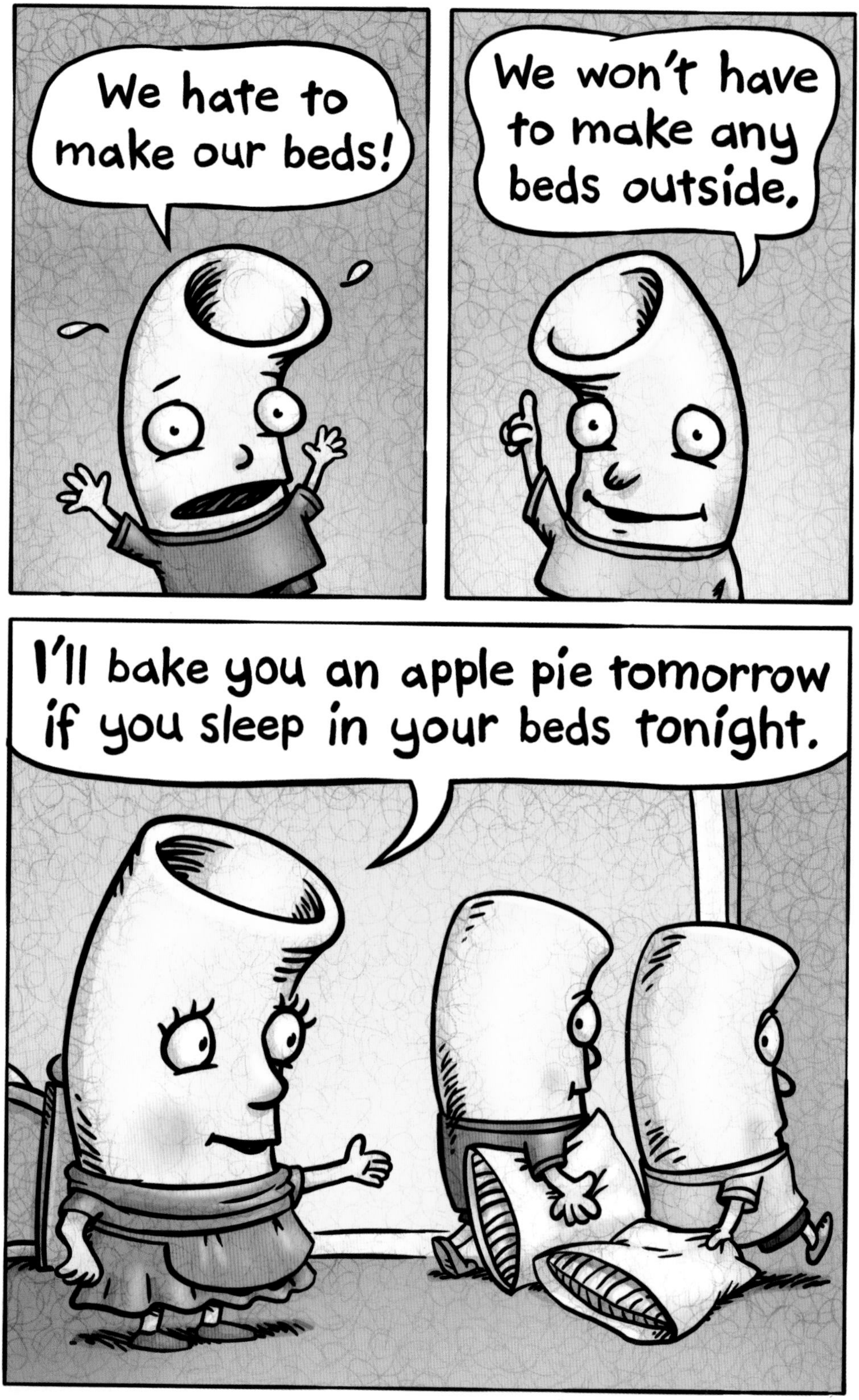
We hate to make our beds!
We won't have to make any beds outside.
I'll bake you an apple pie tomorrow if you sleep in your beds tonight.

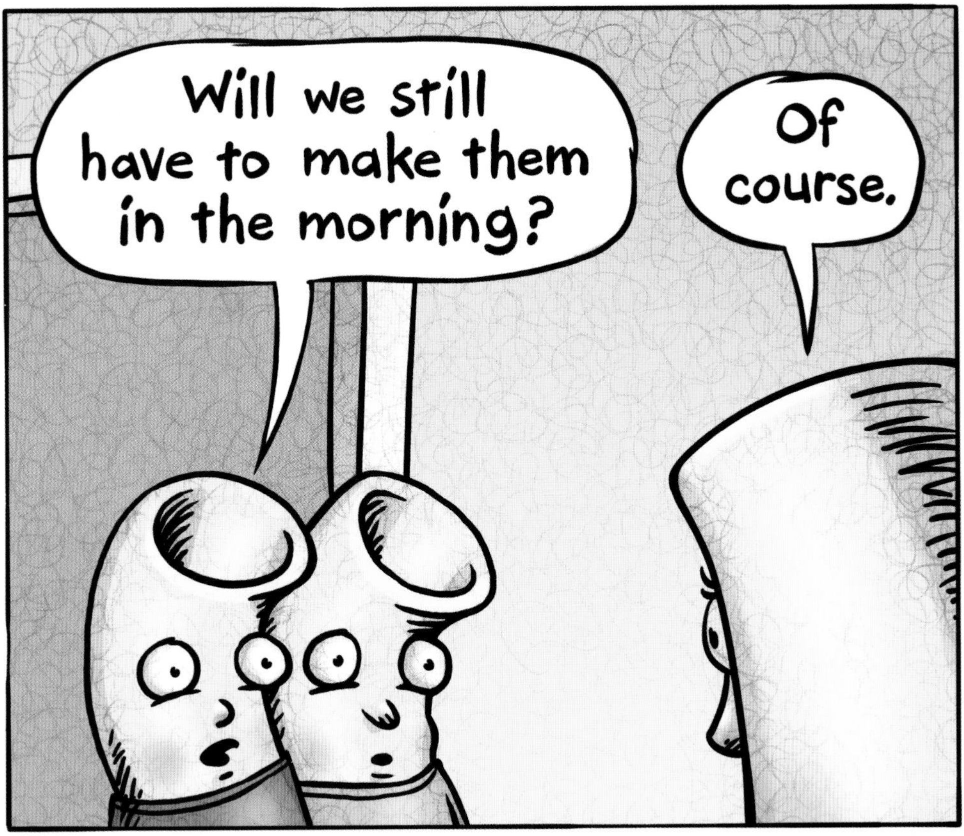
Will we still have to make them in the morning?
Of course.

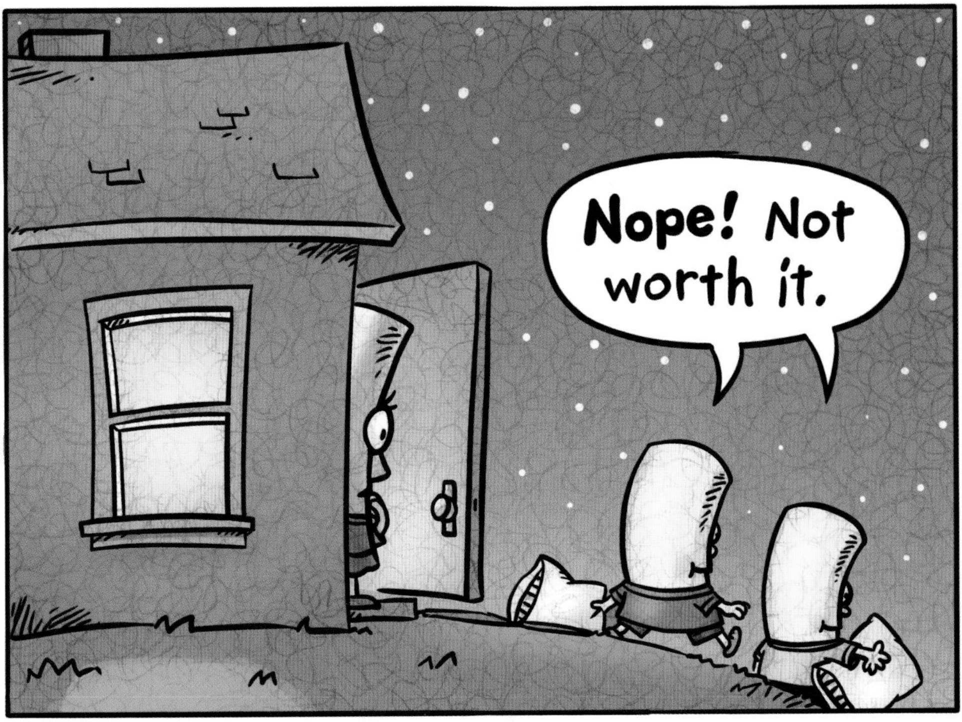
Nope! Not worth it.

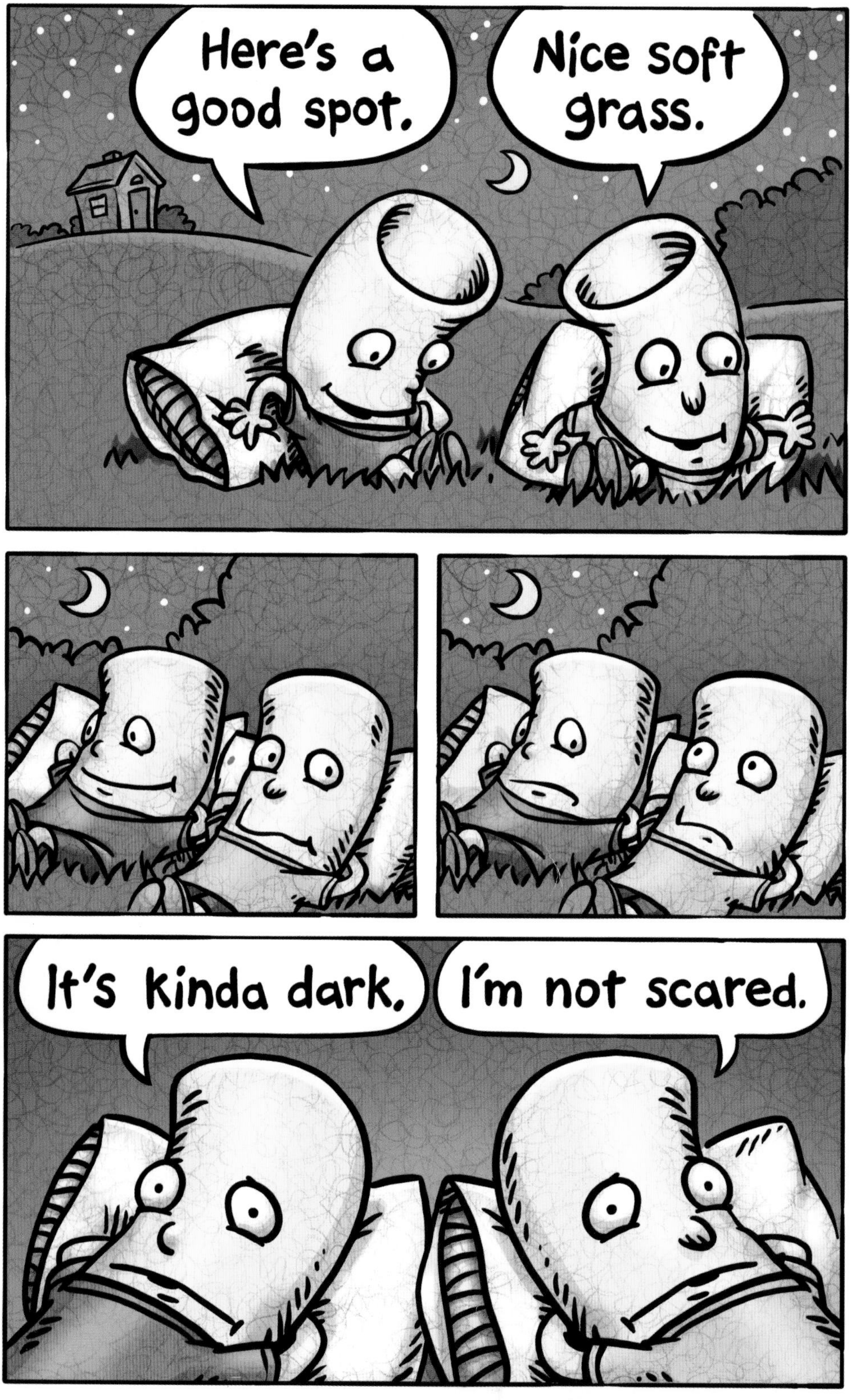
Here's a good spot.
Nice soft grass.
It's kinda dark.
I'm not scared.

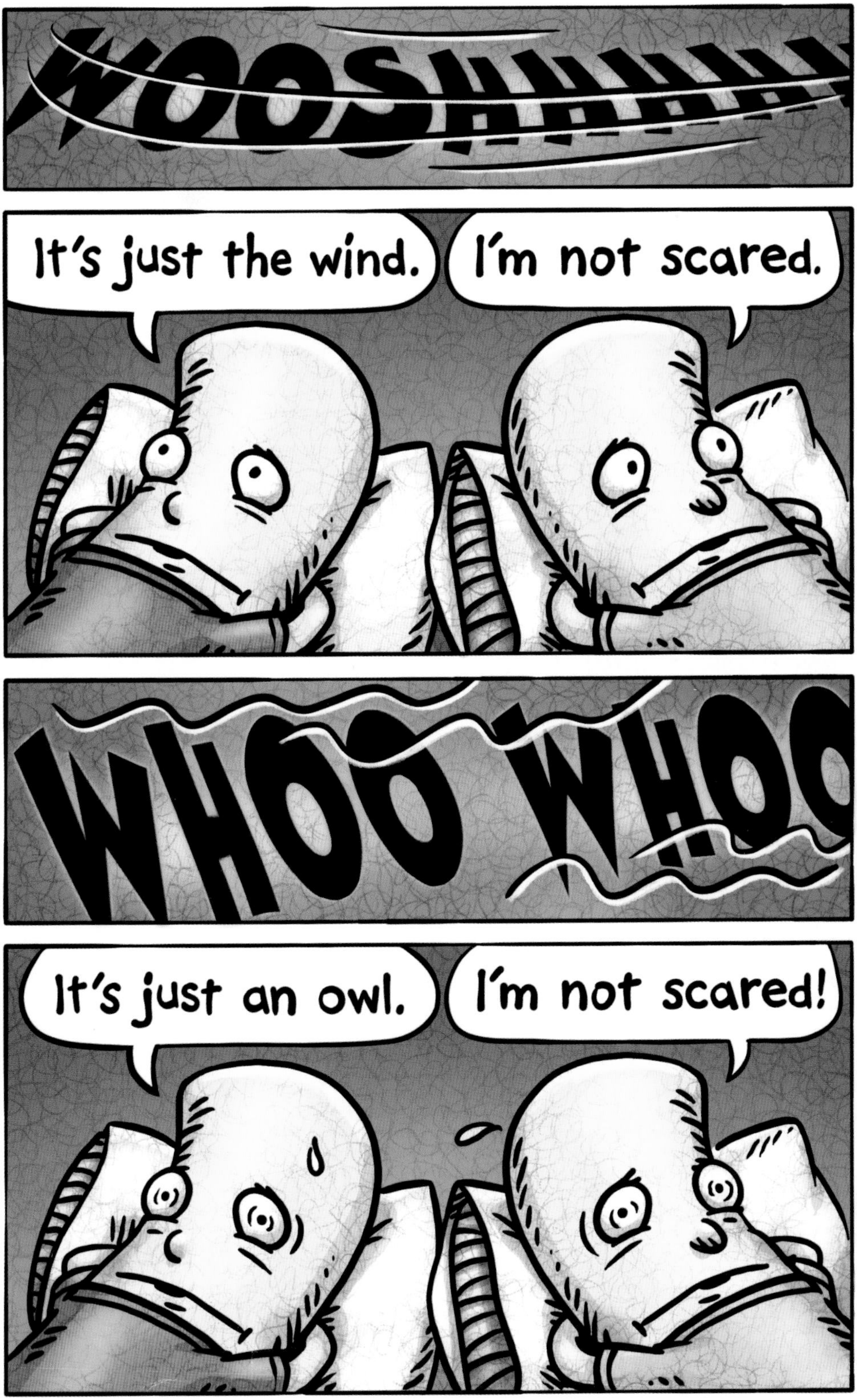
WOOSHHHH
It's just the wind.
I'm not scared.
WHOO WHOO
It's just an owl.
I'm not scared!

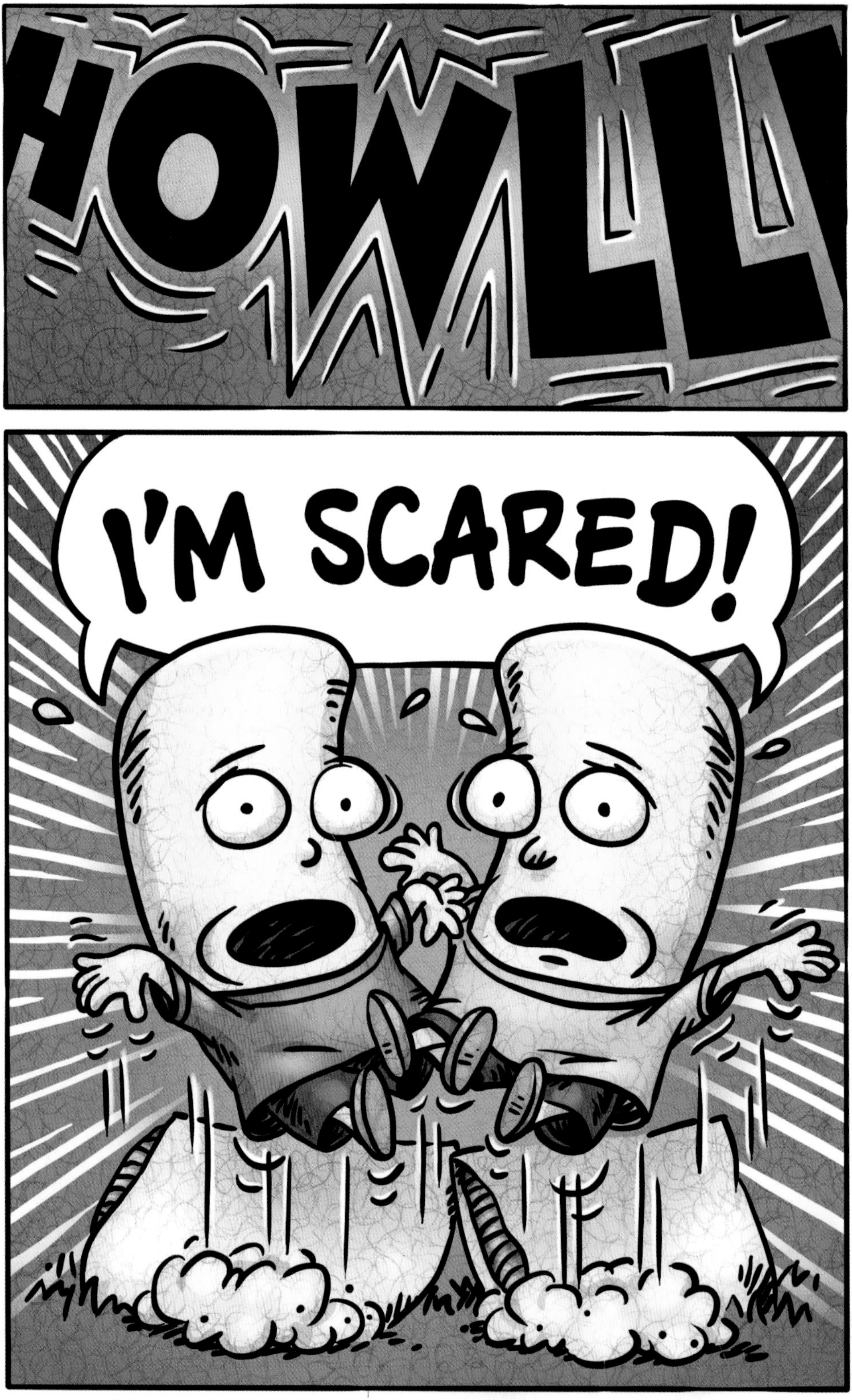
HOWLL
I'M SCARED!

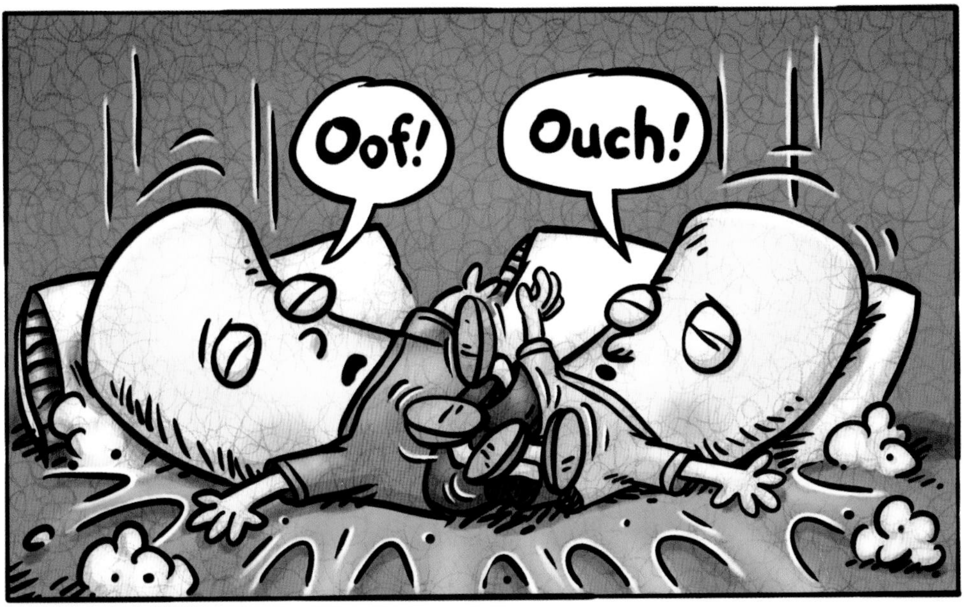
Oof!
Ouch!

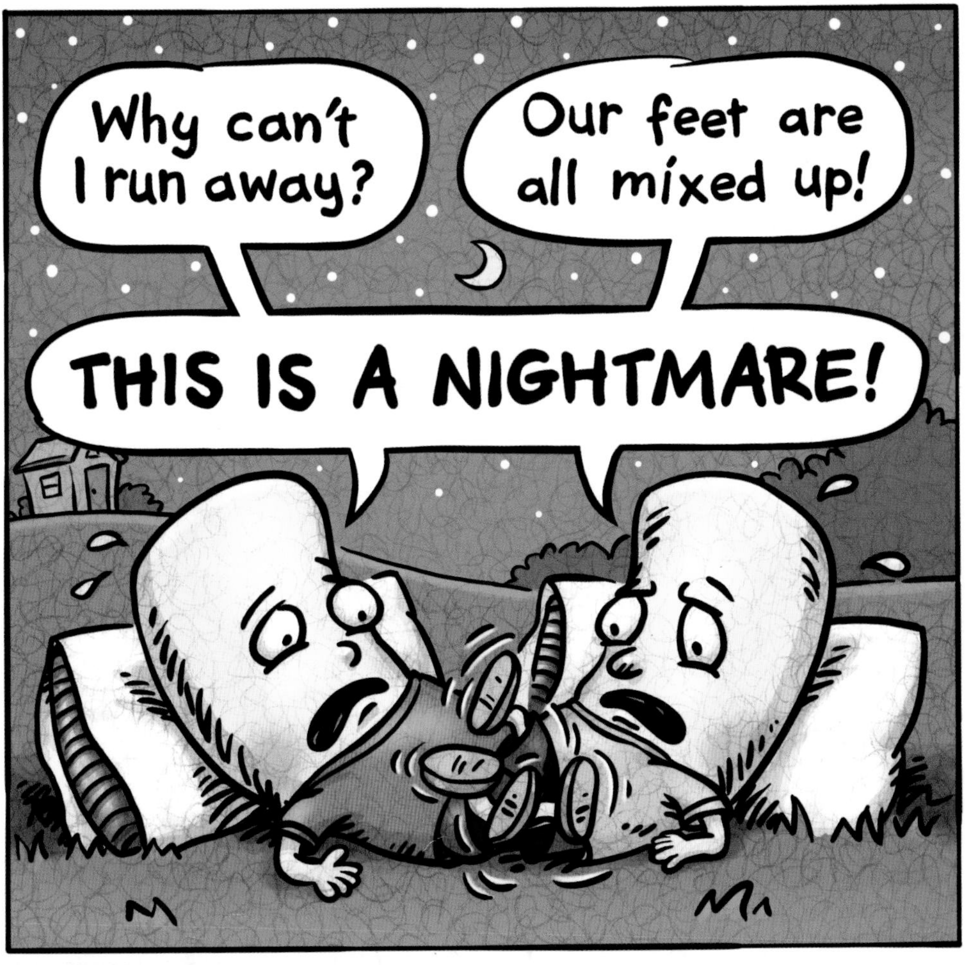
Why can't I run away?
Our feet are all mixed up!
THIS IS A NIGHTMARE!

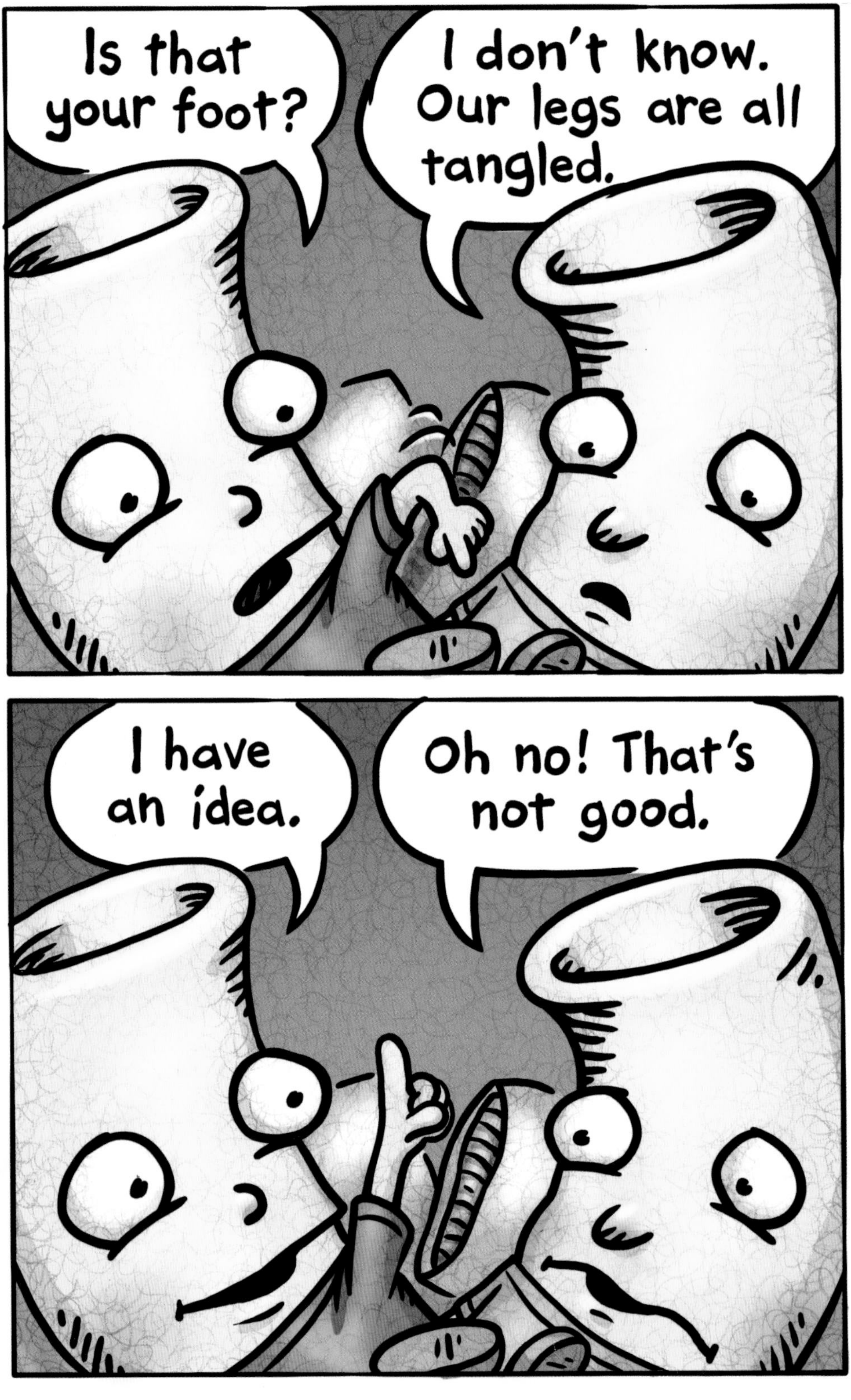
Is that your foot?
I don't know. Our legs are all tangled.
I have an idea.
Oh no! That's not good.

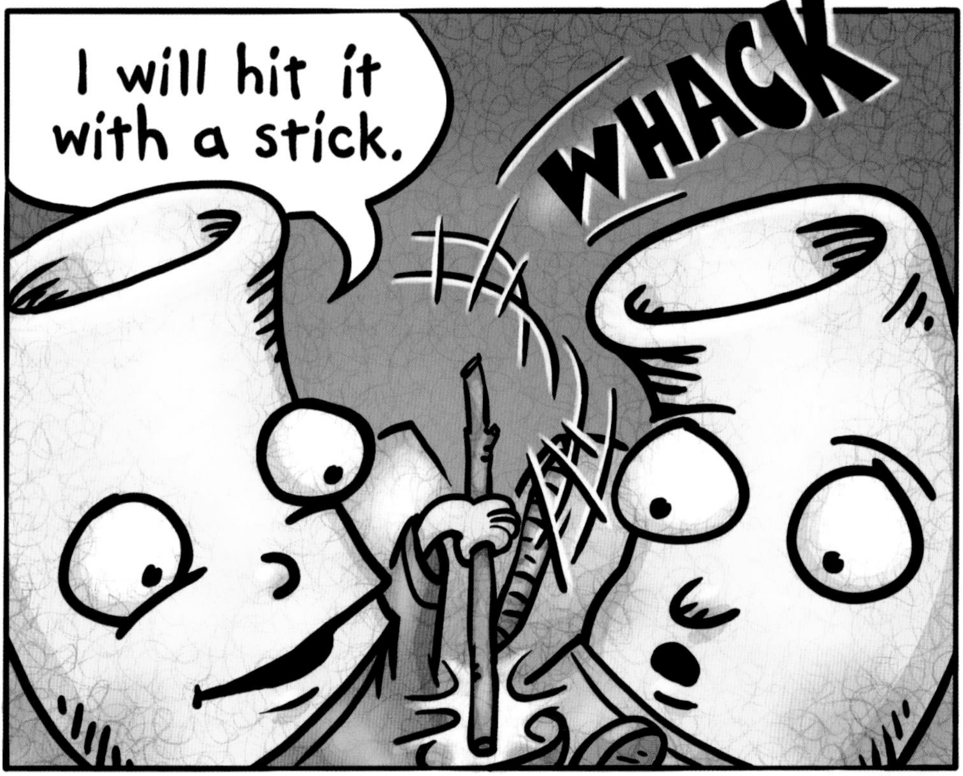
I will hit it with a stick.
WHACK

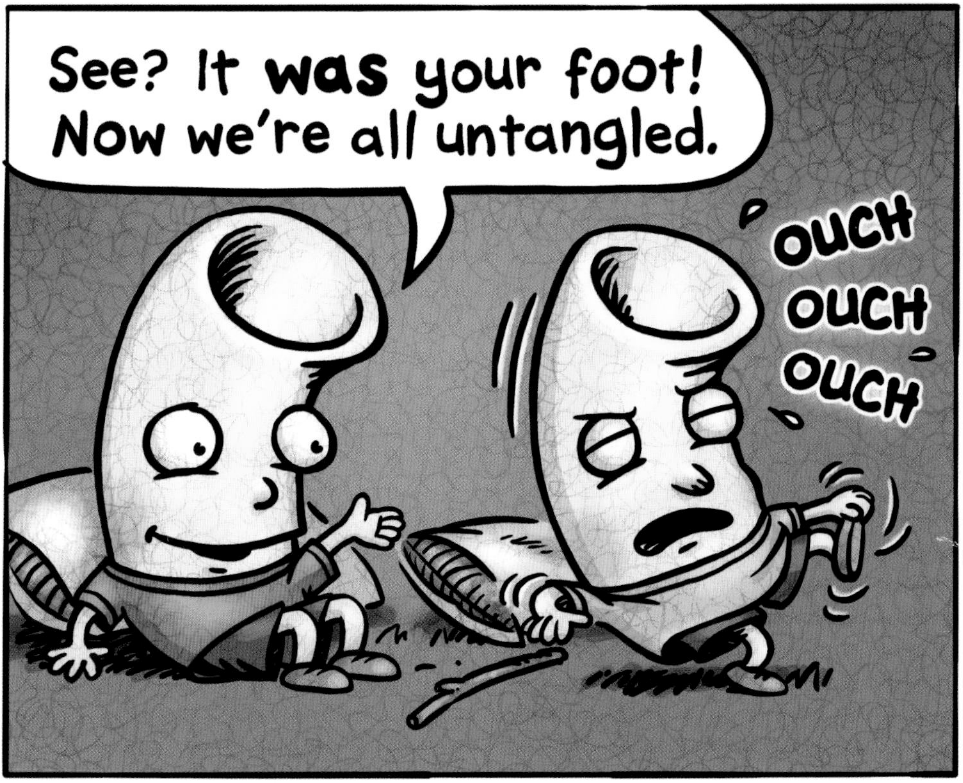
See? It **was** your foot! Now we're all untangled.
OUCH
OUCH
OUCH

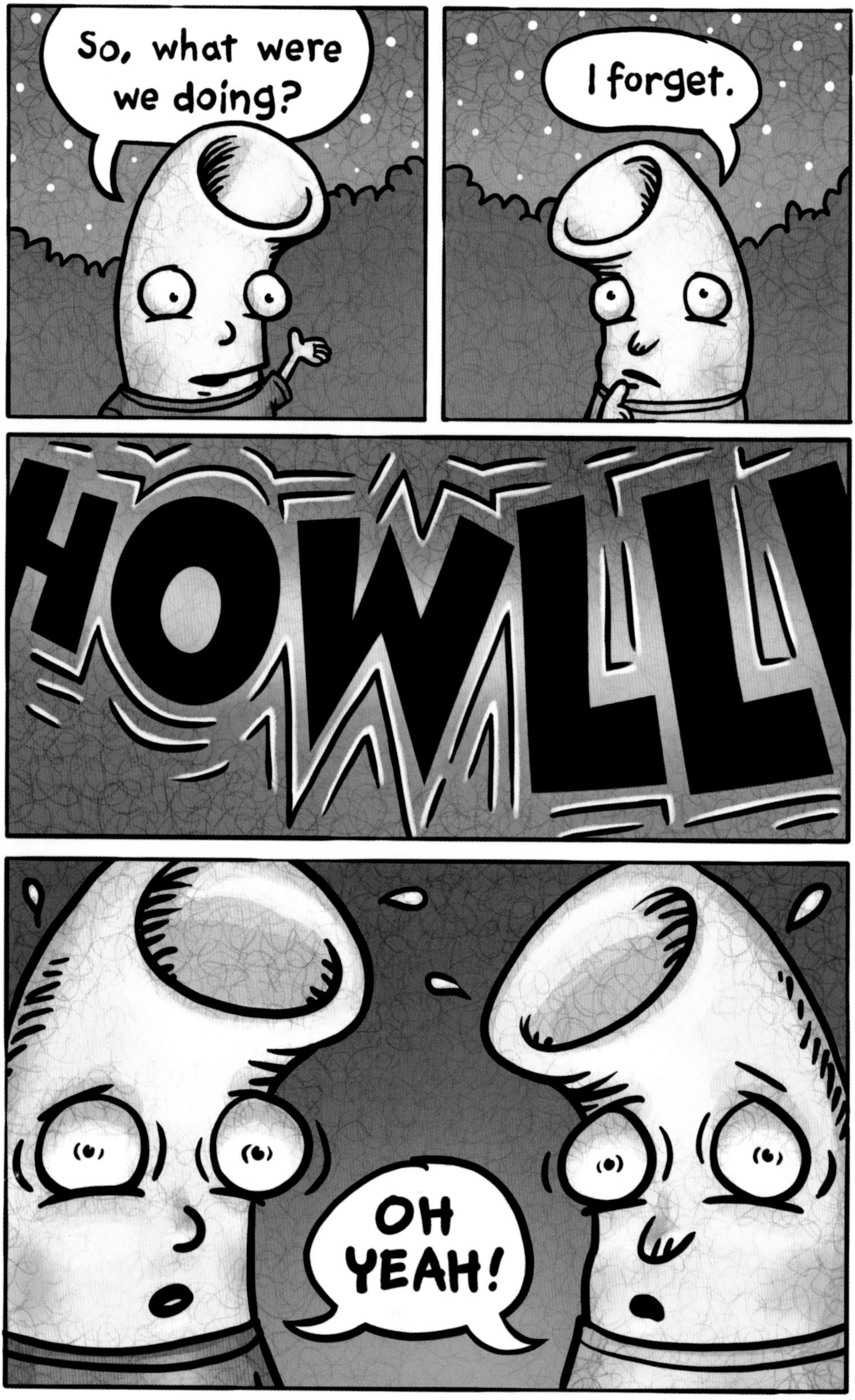

So, what were we doing?
I forget.
HOWLLL
OH YEAH!

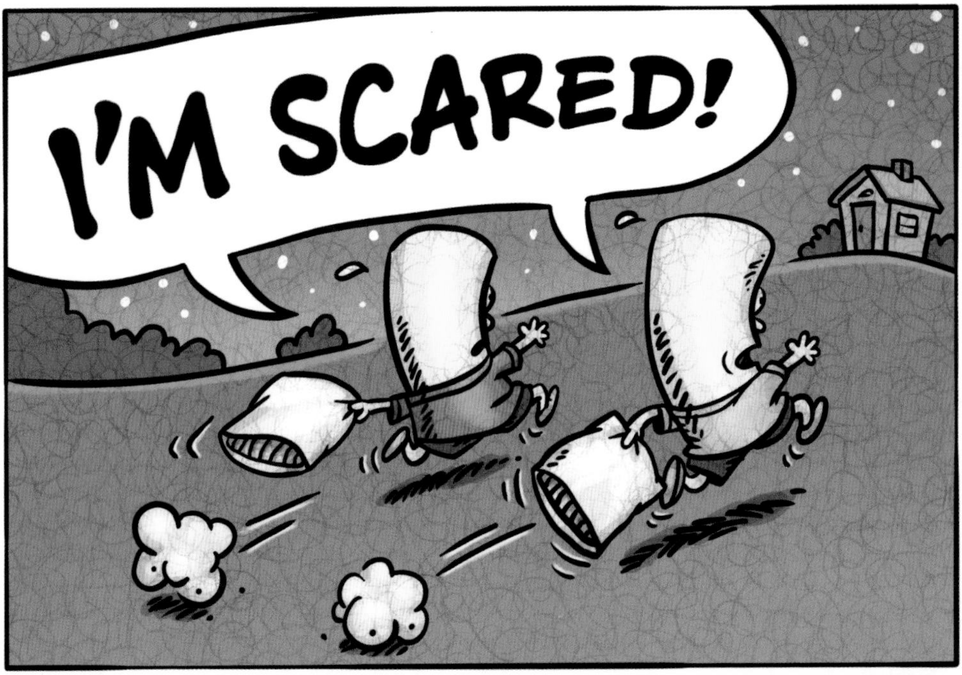
I'M SCARED!

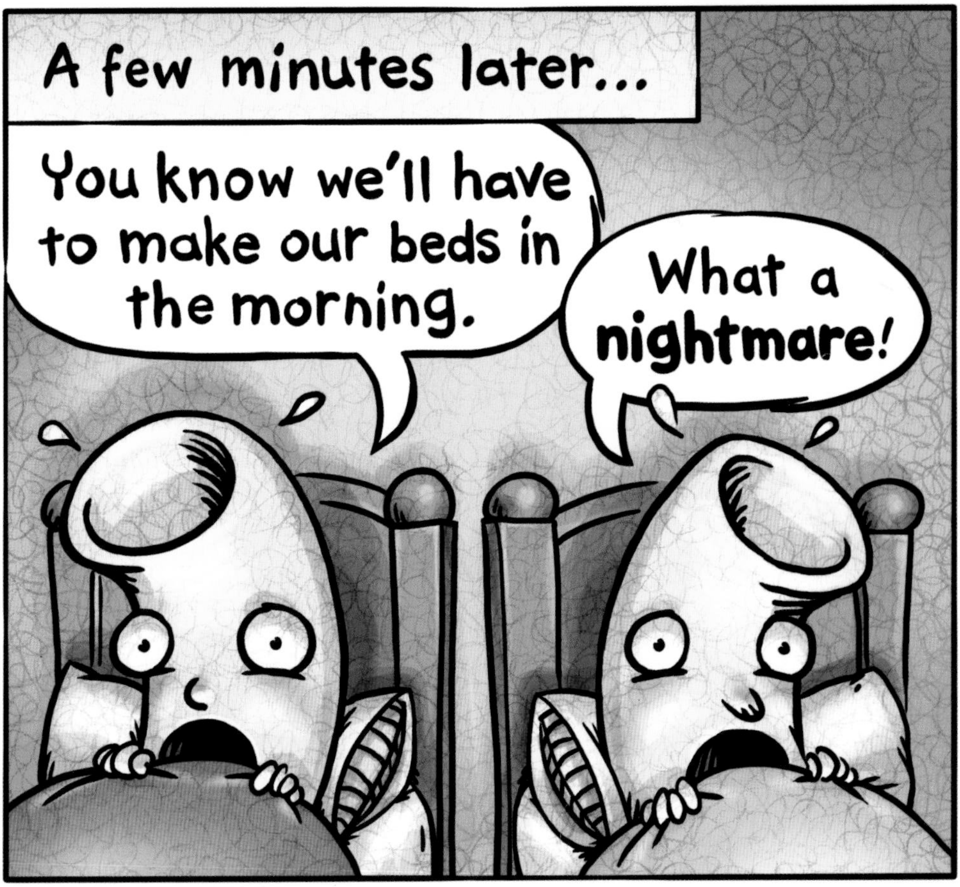
A few minutes later...
You know we'll have to make our beds in the morning.
What a **nightmare**!

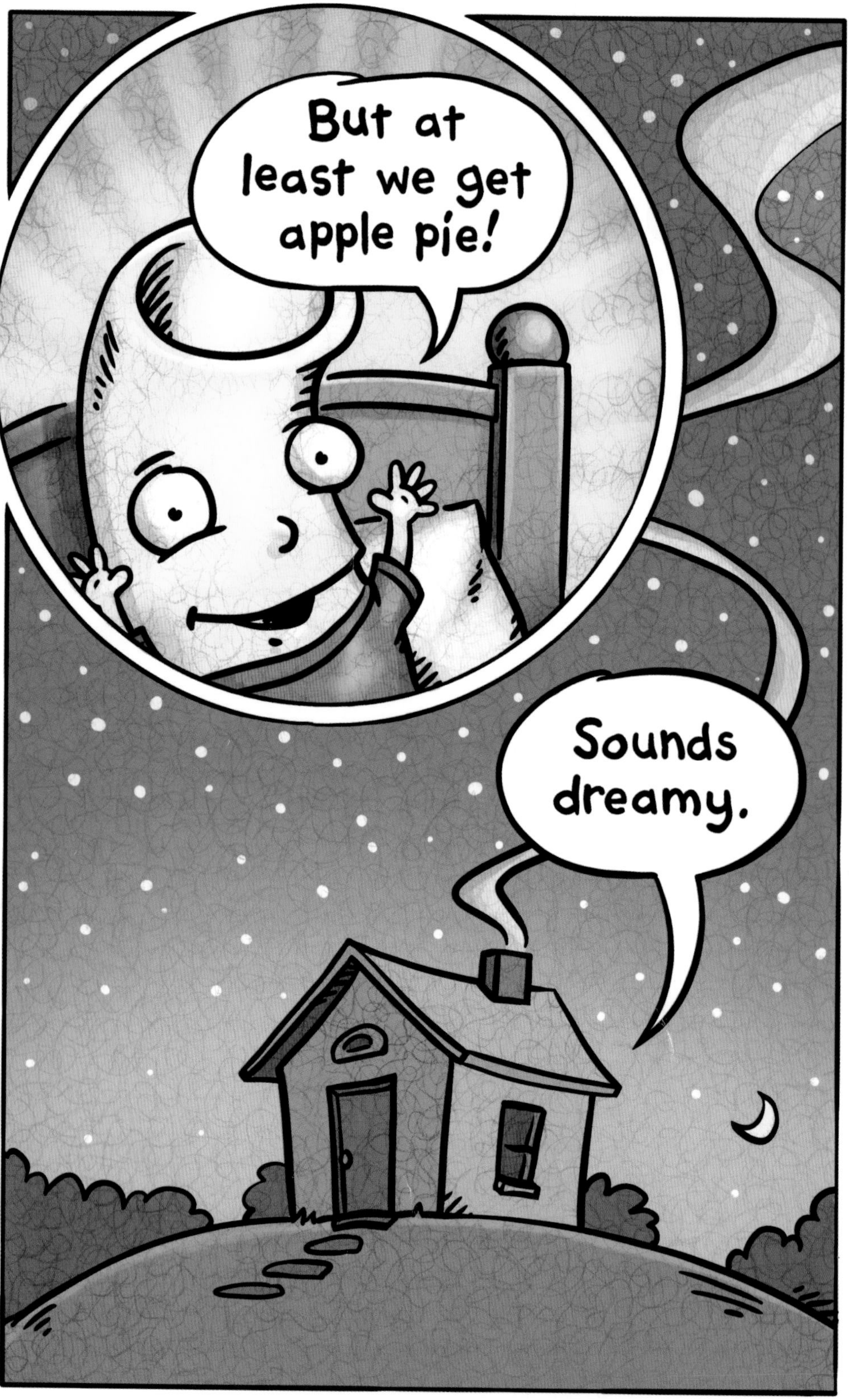
But at least we get apple pie!
Sounds dreamy.

NOODLEHEAD NIGHTMARES

CHAPTER 2
THE BEST DREAM

Next day, Mac and Mac were outside when they smelled...

APPLE PIE!

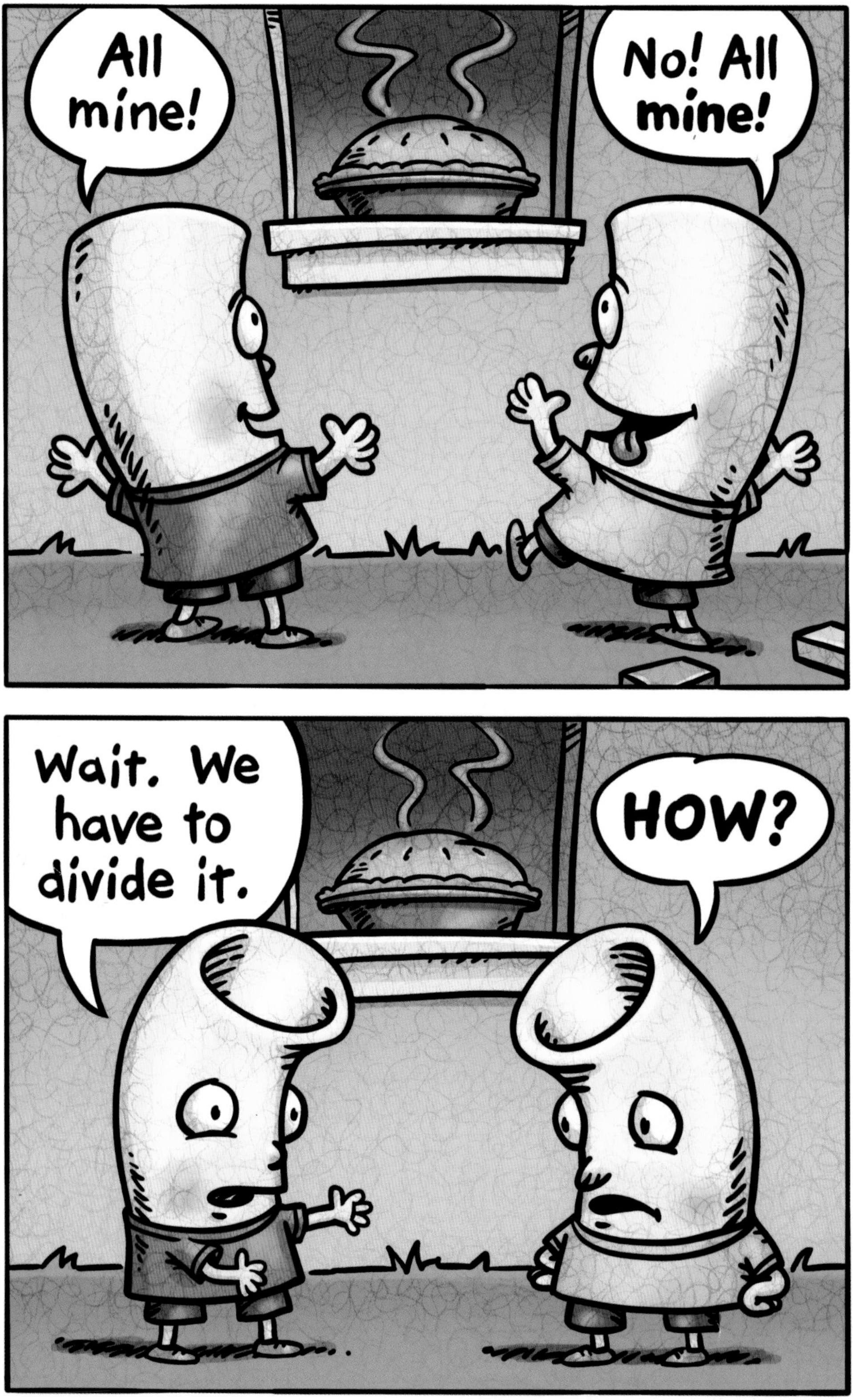
All mine!
No! All mine!
Wait. We have to divide it.
HOW?

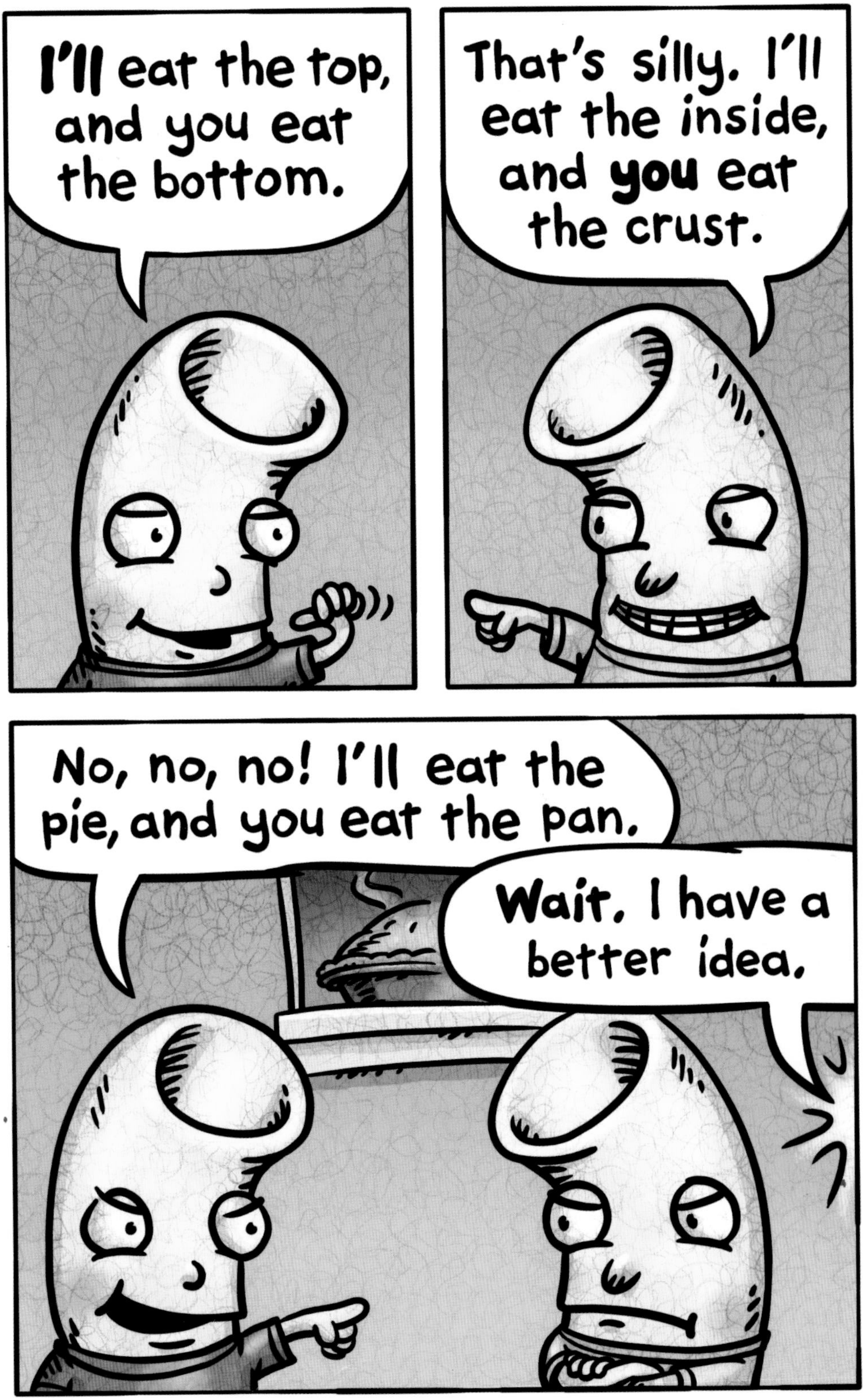
I'll eat the top, and you eat the bottom.
That's silly. I'll eat the inside, and **you** eat the crust.
No, no, no! I'll eat the pie, and you eat the pan.
Wait. I have a better idea.

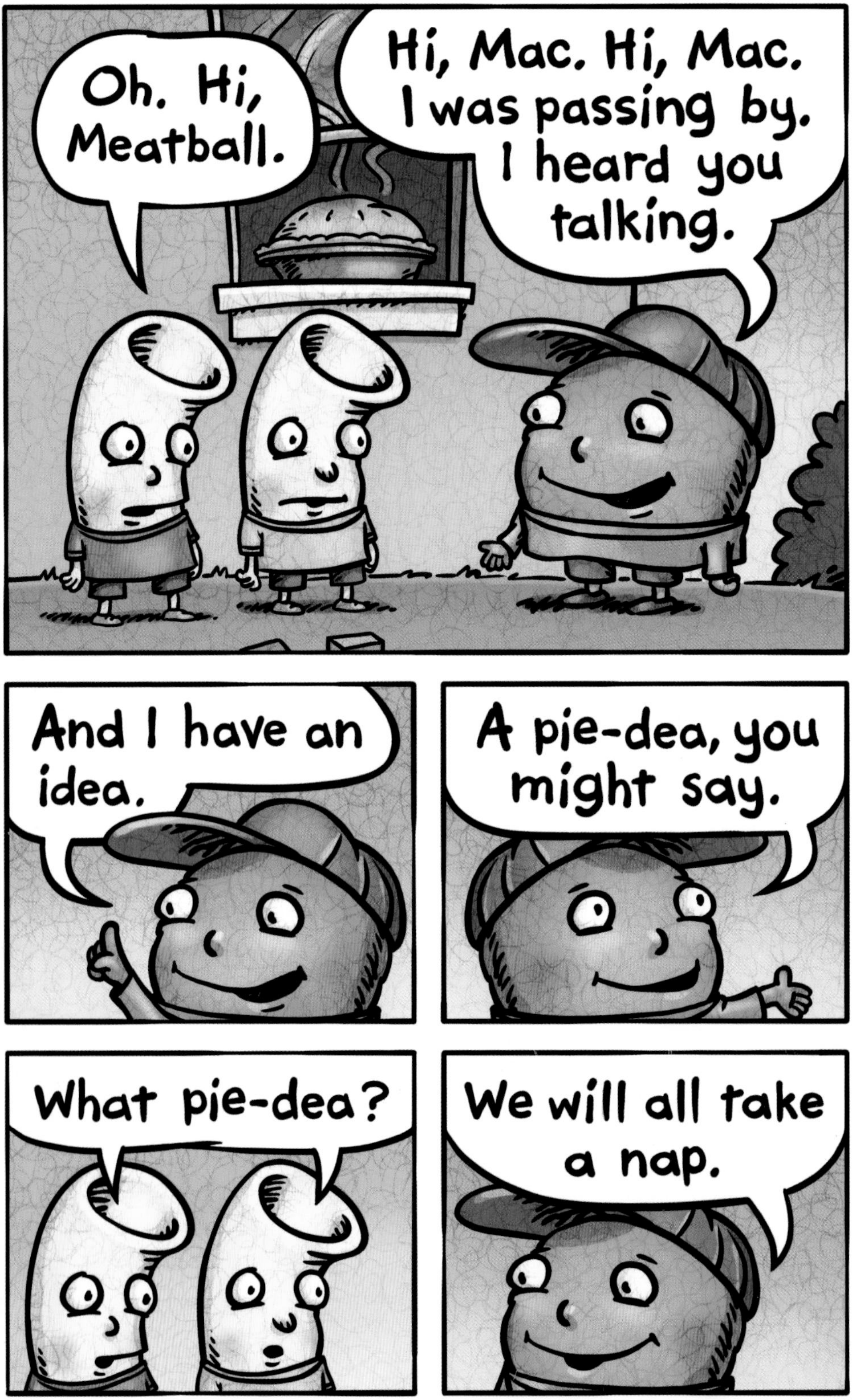
Oh. Hi, Meatball.
Hi, Mac. Hi, Mac. I was passing by. I heard you talking.
And I have an idea.
A pie-dea, you might say.
What pie-dea?
We will all take a nap.

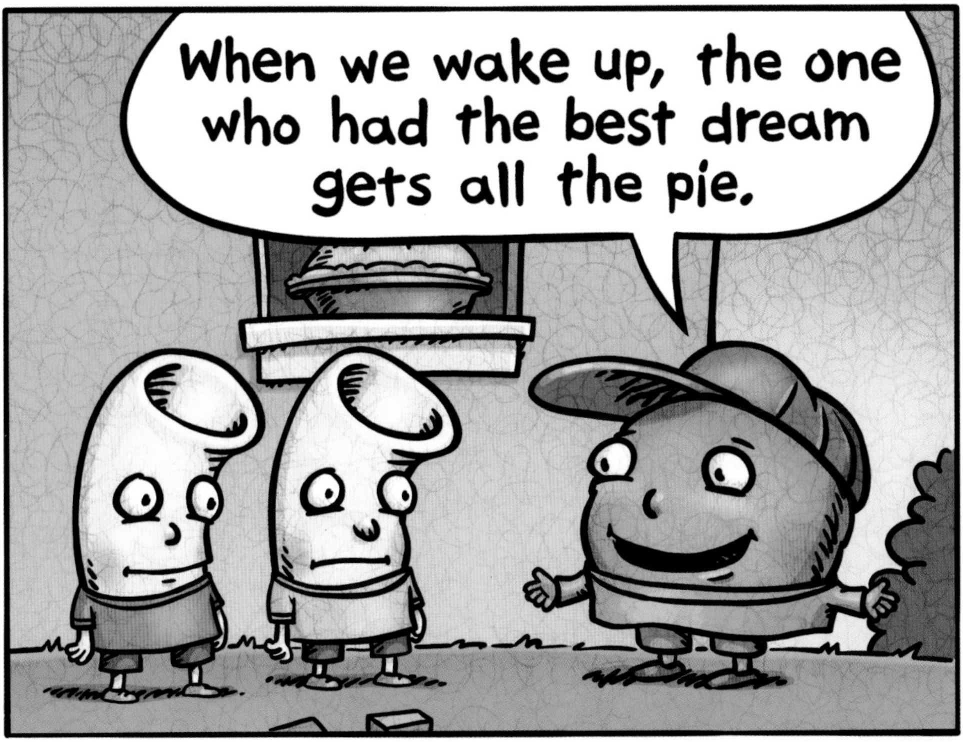
When we wake up, the one who had the best dream gets all the pie.

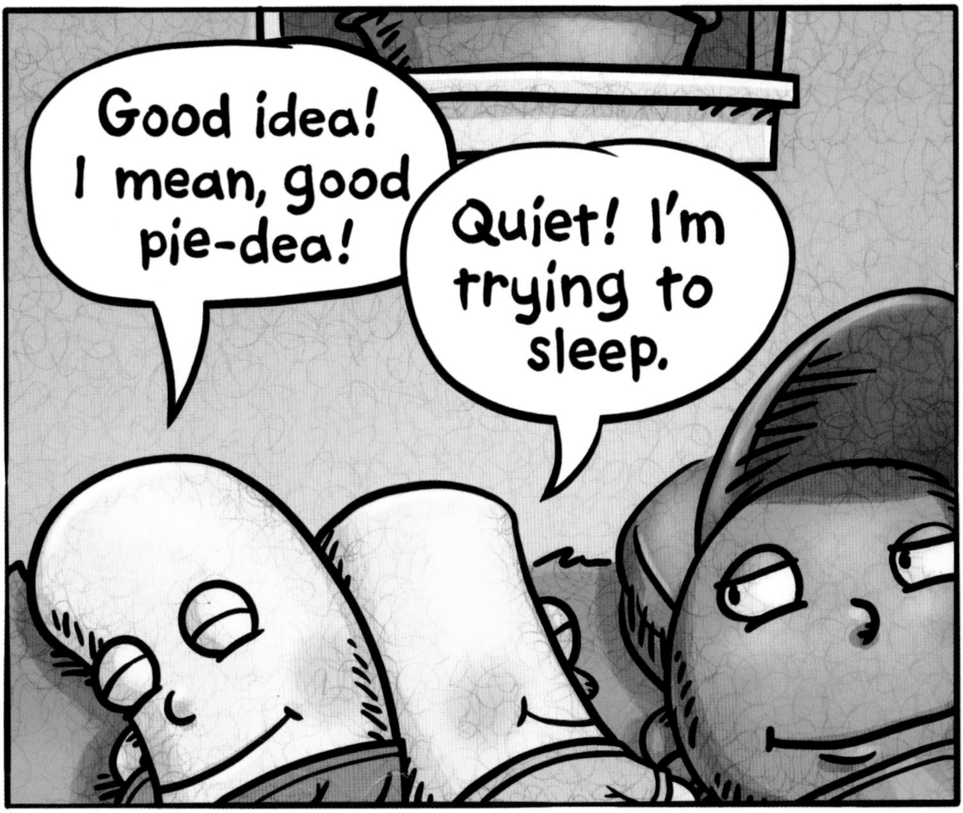
Good idea! I mean, good pie-dea!
Quiet! I'm trying to sleep.

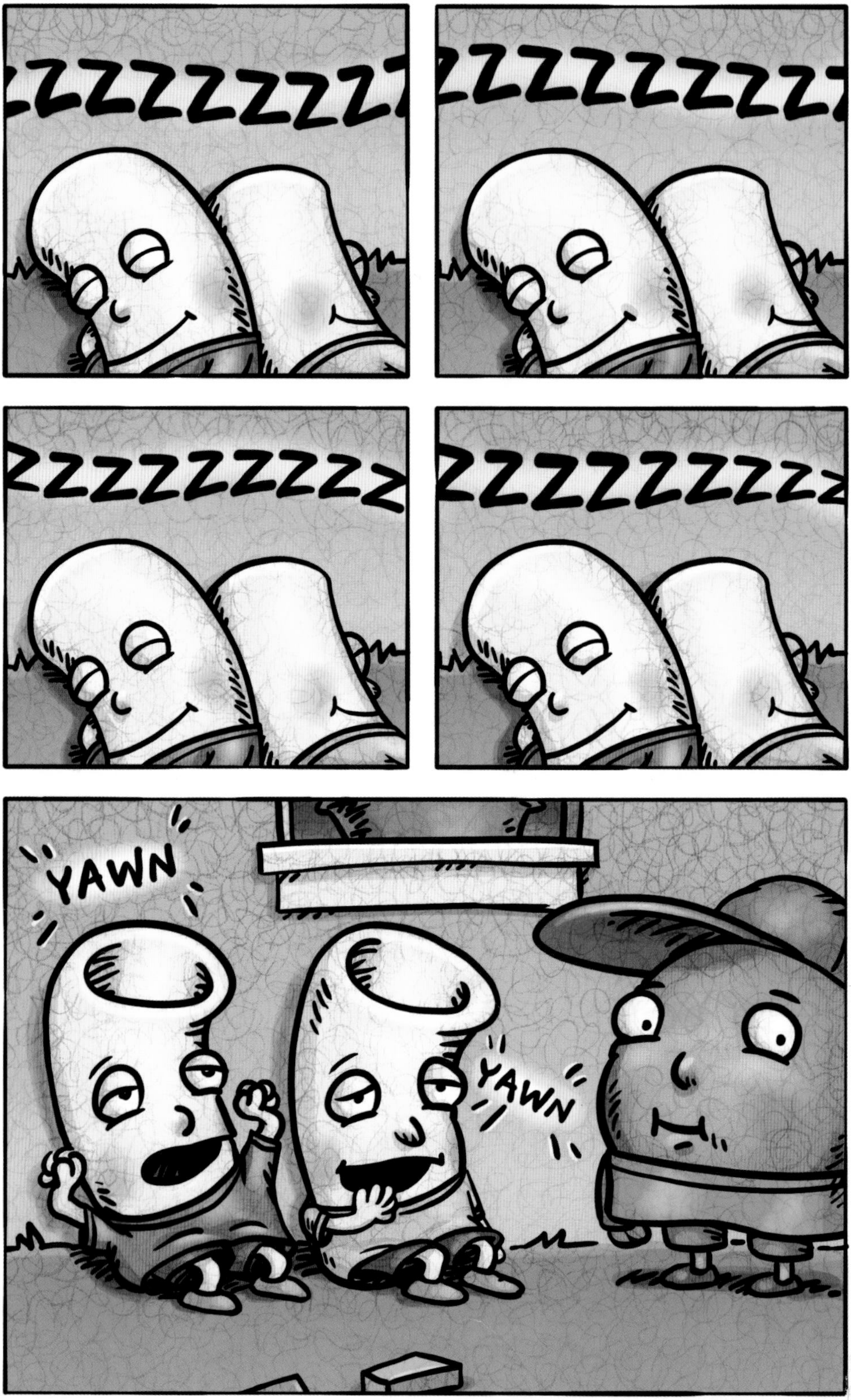
ZZZZZZZZZ
ZZZZZZZZZ
ZZZZZZZZZZ
ZZZZZZZZZZ
YAWN
YAWN

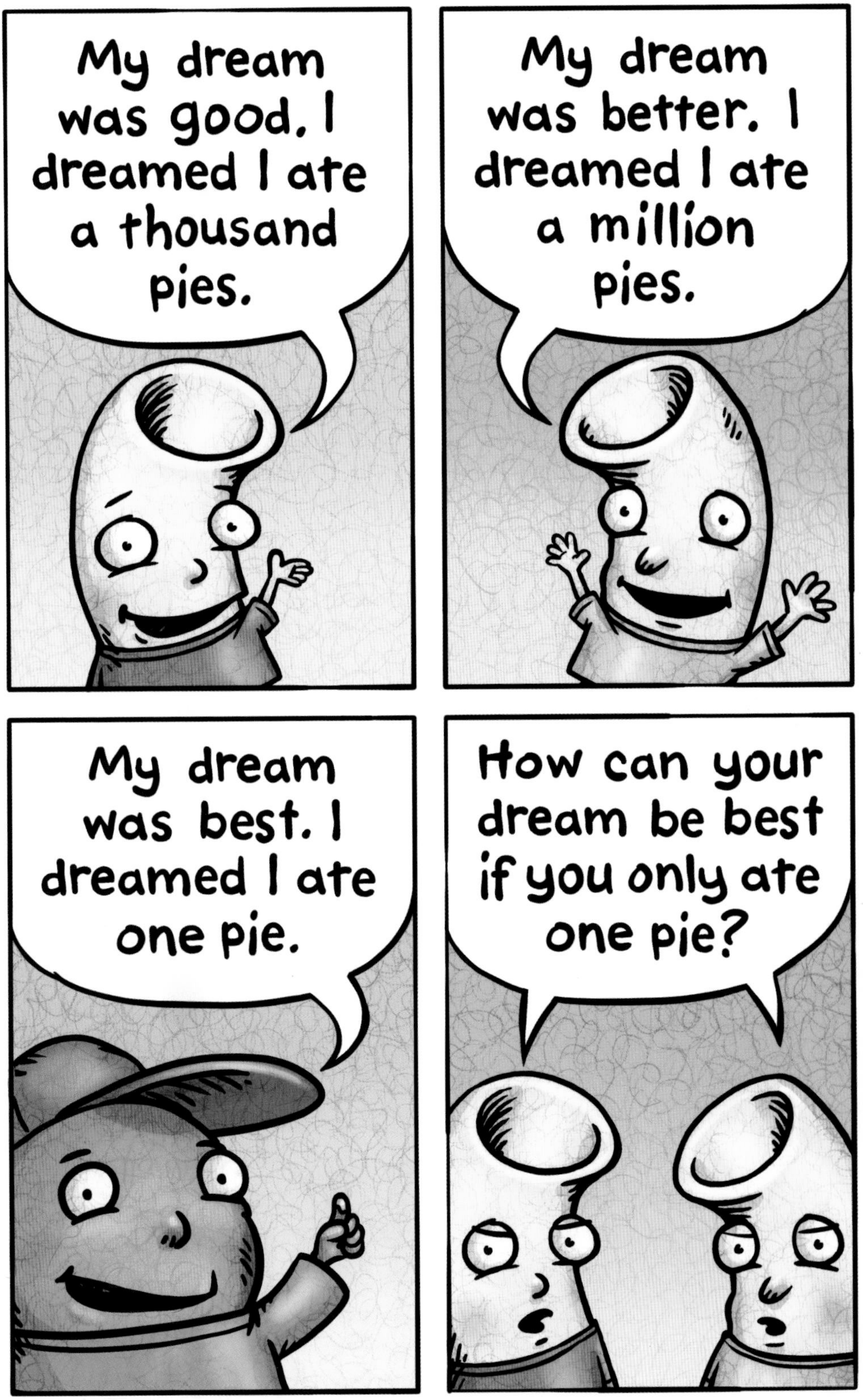
My dream was good. I dreamed I ate a thousand pies.
My dream was better. I dreamed I ate a million pies.
My dream was best. I dreamed I ate one pie.
How can your dream be best if you only ate one pie?

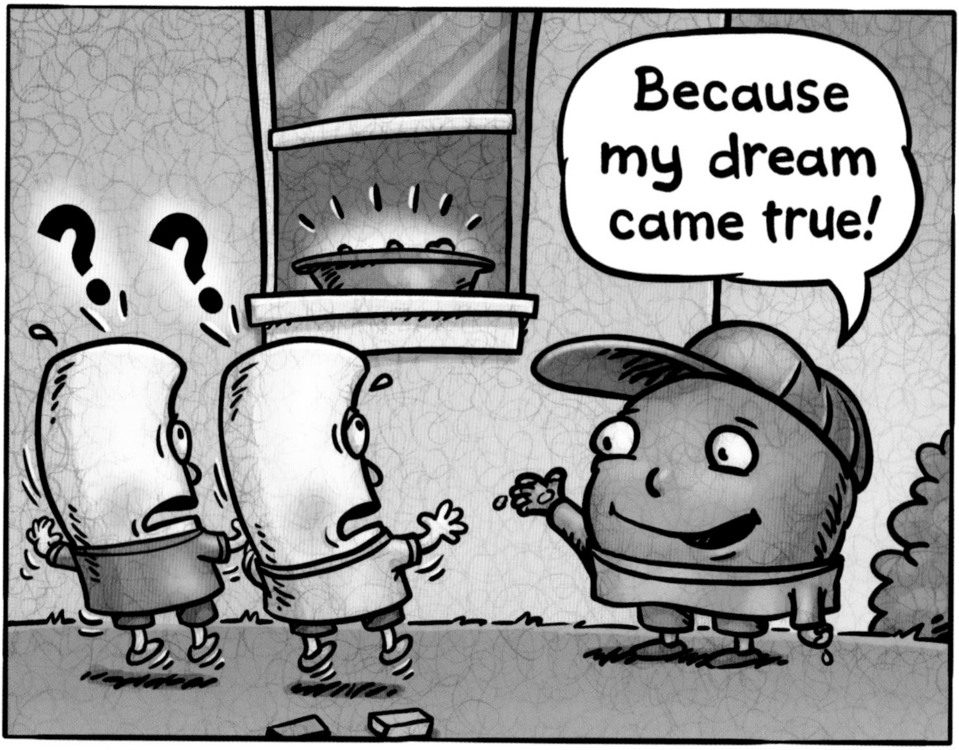
Because my dream came true!

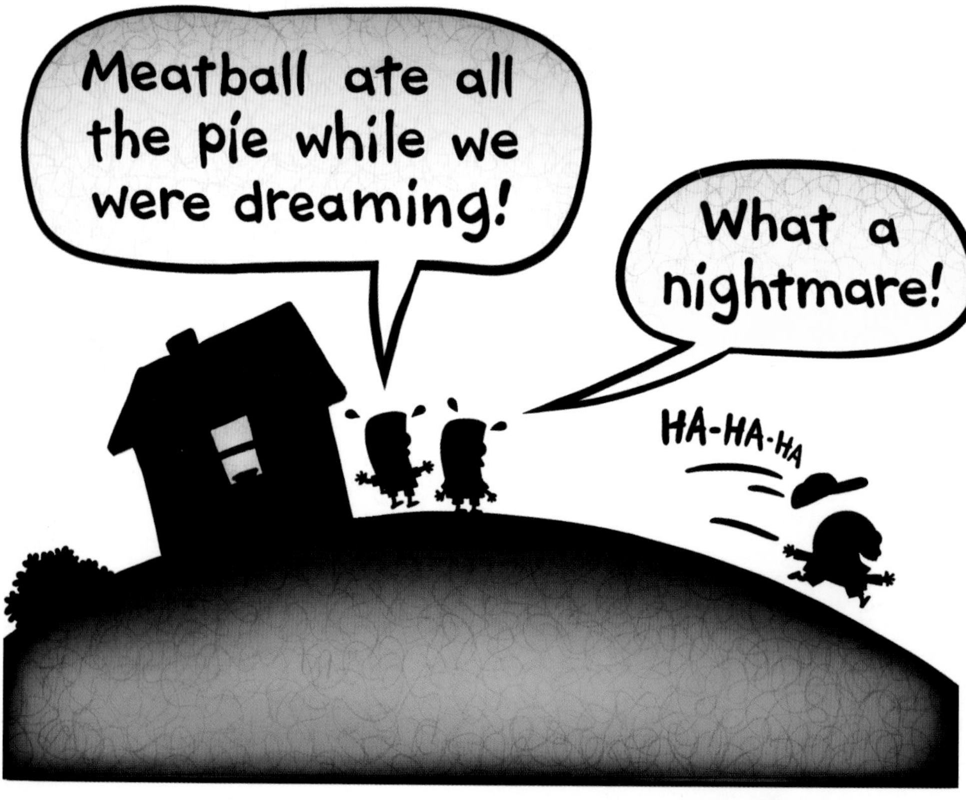
Meatball ate all the pie while we were dreaming!
What a nightmare!
HA-HA-HA

NOODLEHEAD NIGHTMARES

CHAPTER 3

BEDTIME FOR NOODLEHEADS

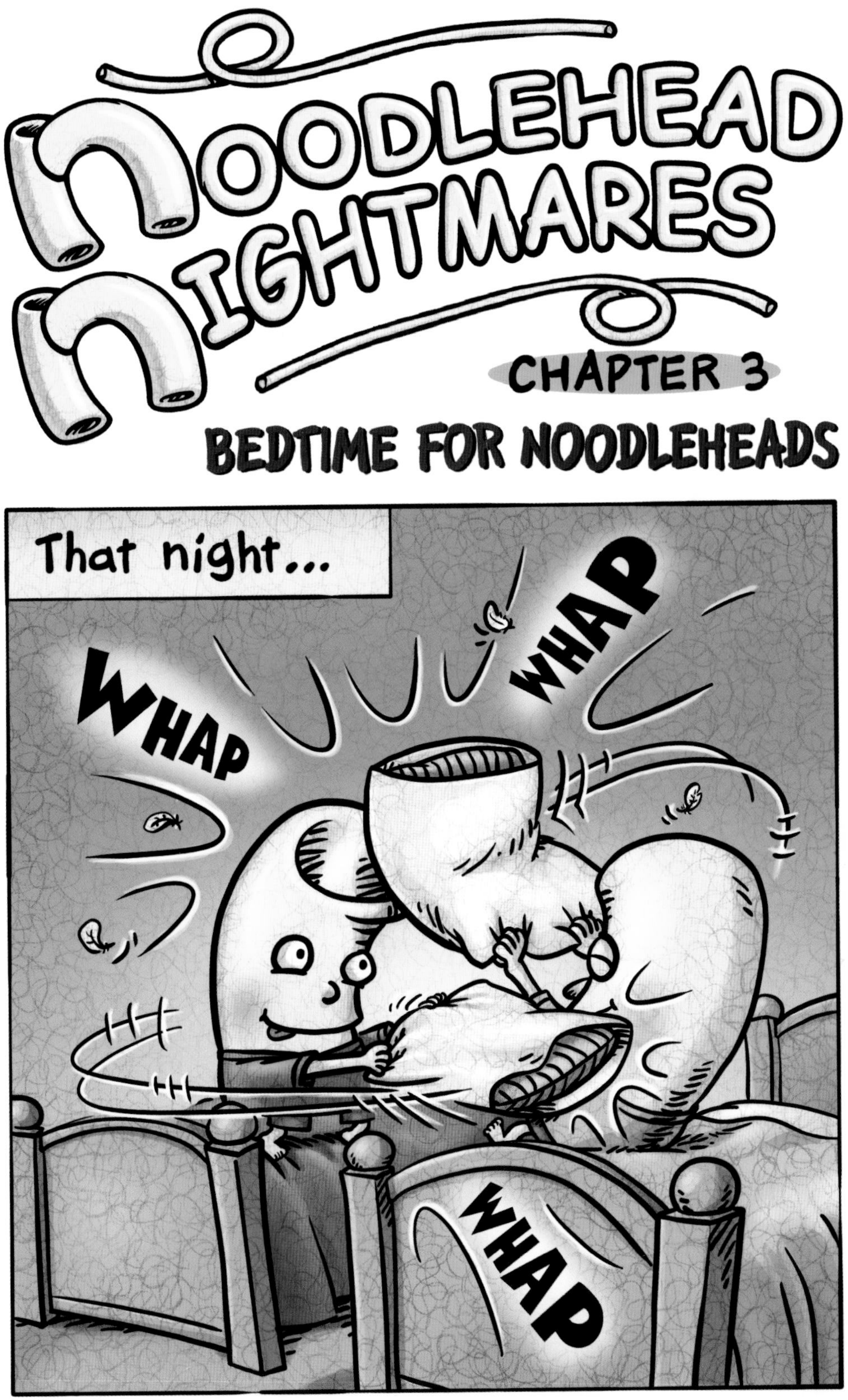

That night...
WHAP
WHAP
WHAP

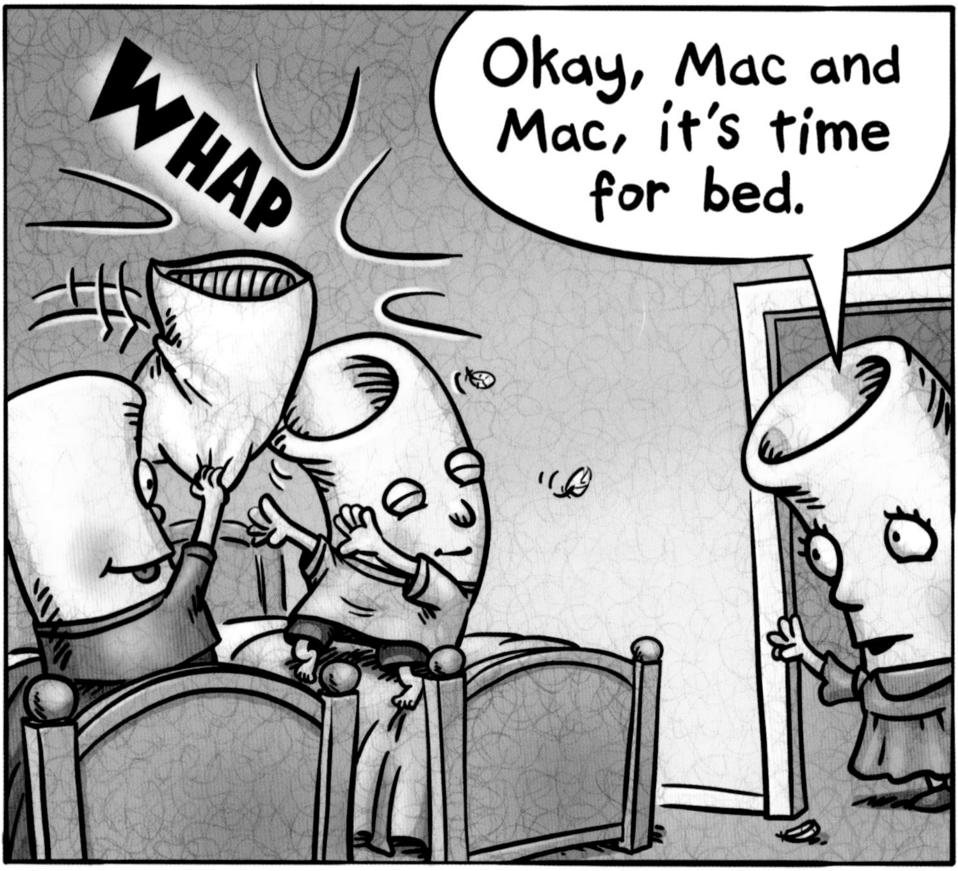
WHAP
Okay, Mac and Mac, it's time for bed.

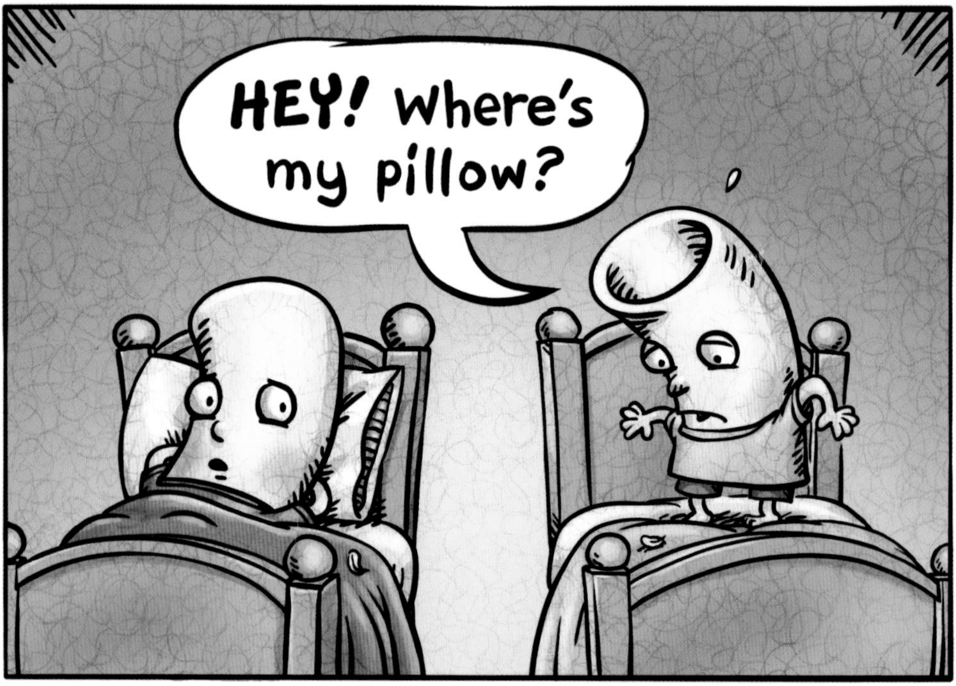
HEY! Where's my pillow?

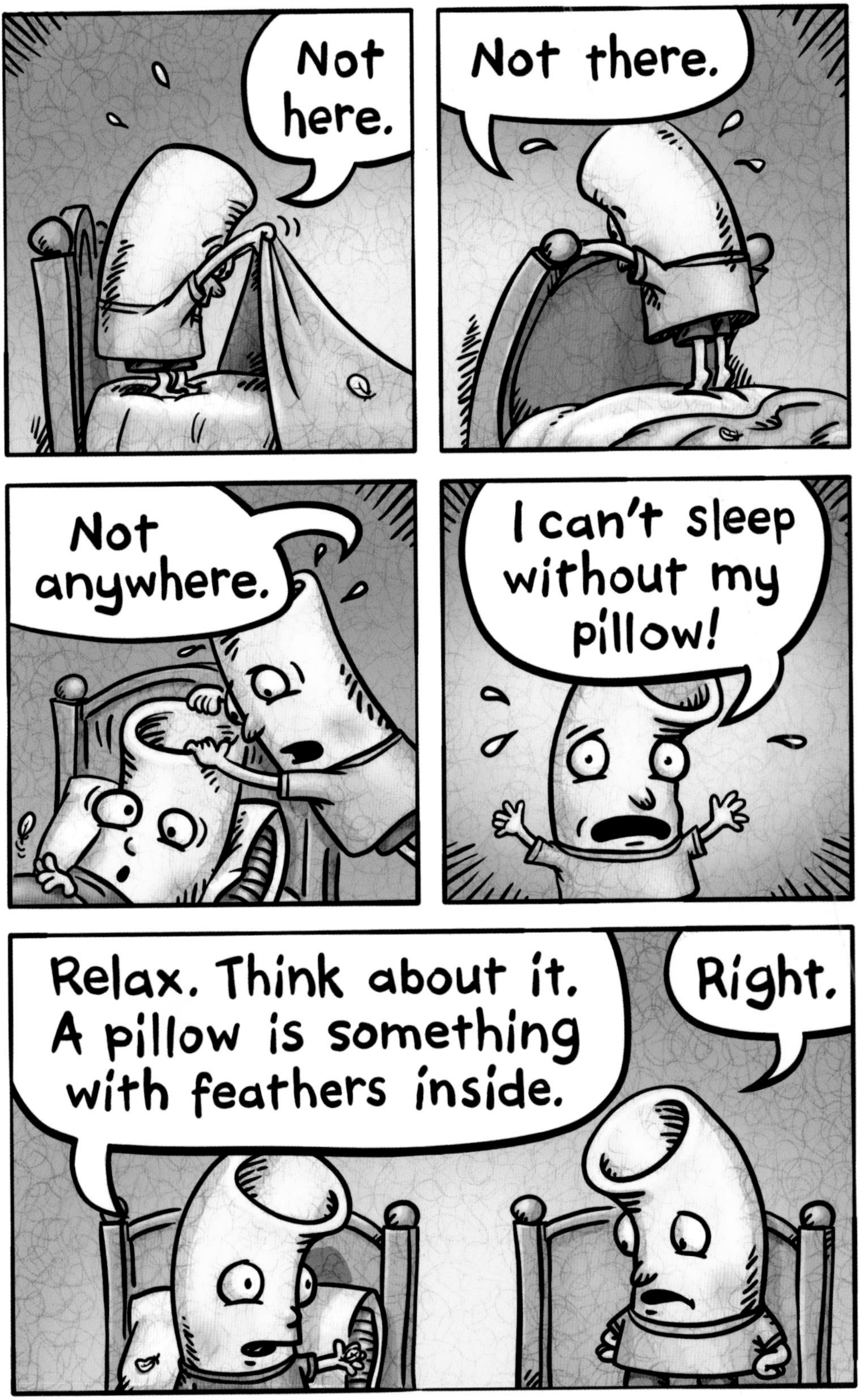
Not here.
Not there.
Not anywhere.
I can't sleep without my pillow!
Relax. Think about it. A pillow is something with feathers inside.
Right.

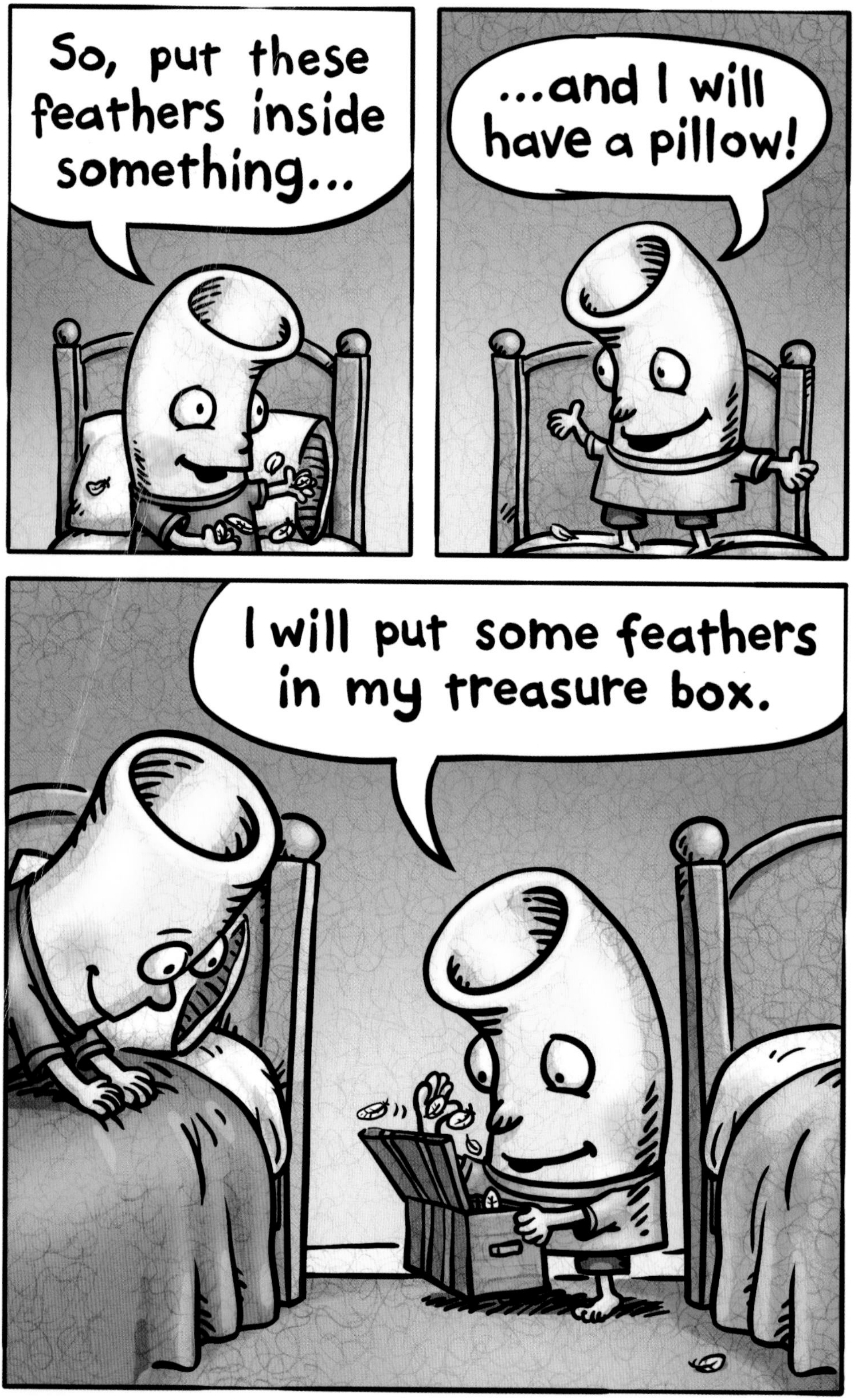
So, put these feathers inside something...
...and I will have a pillow!
I will put some feathers in my treasure box.

Mac was not comfortable, but he was tired.

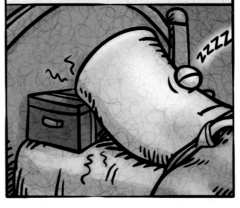

He tossed and he turned, and finally he slept.

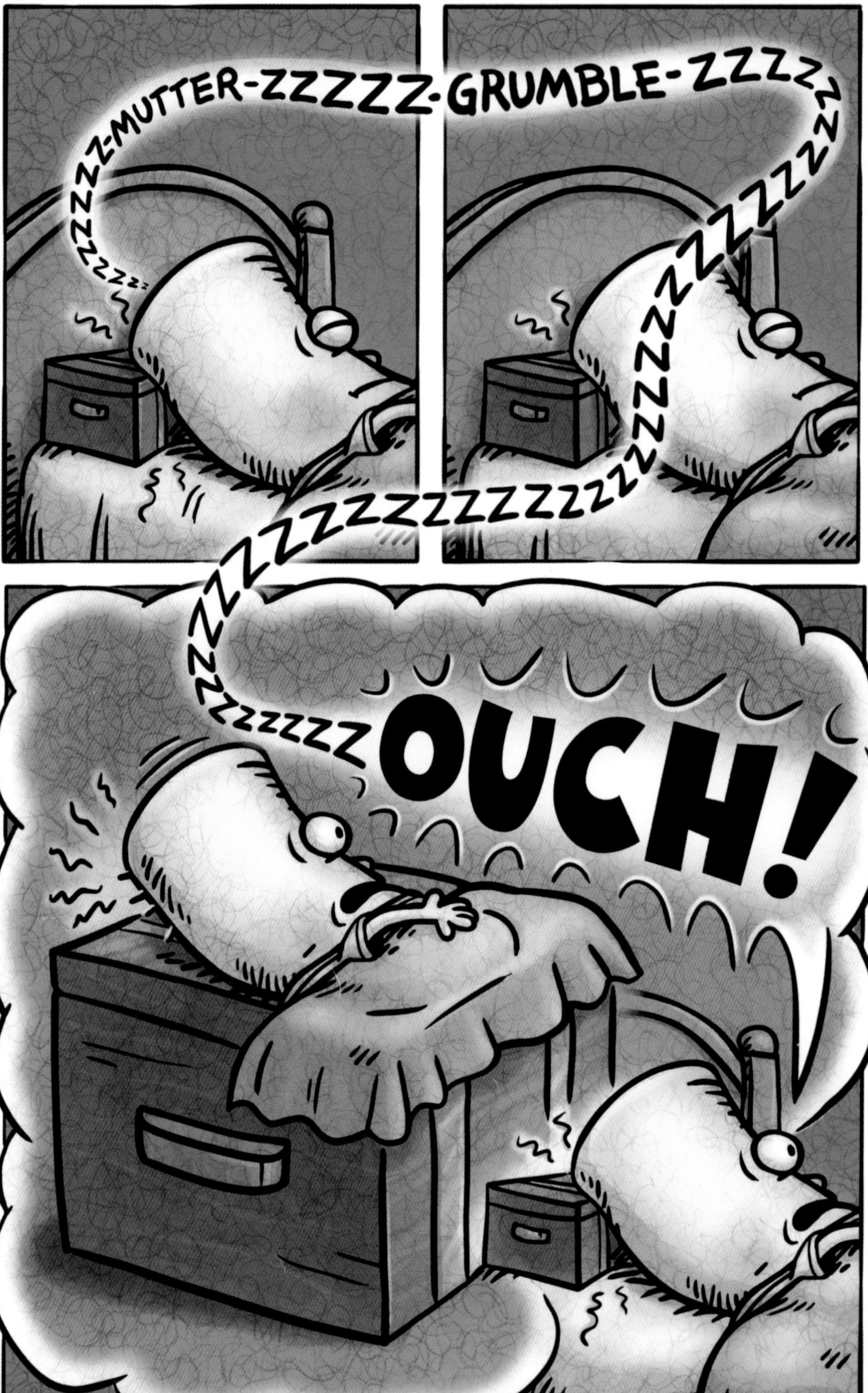

ZZZZZZZZZ-MUTTER-ZZZZZZ-GRUMBLE-ZZZZZZZZZZZZZZZZZZZZZZZZZZZZZZZZZZZZZZZZZZZZZZZZZZZZZZZZZZZZ
OUCH!

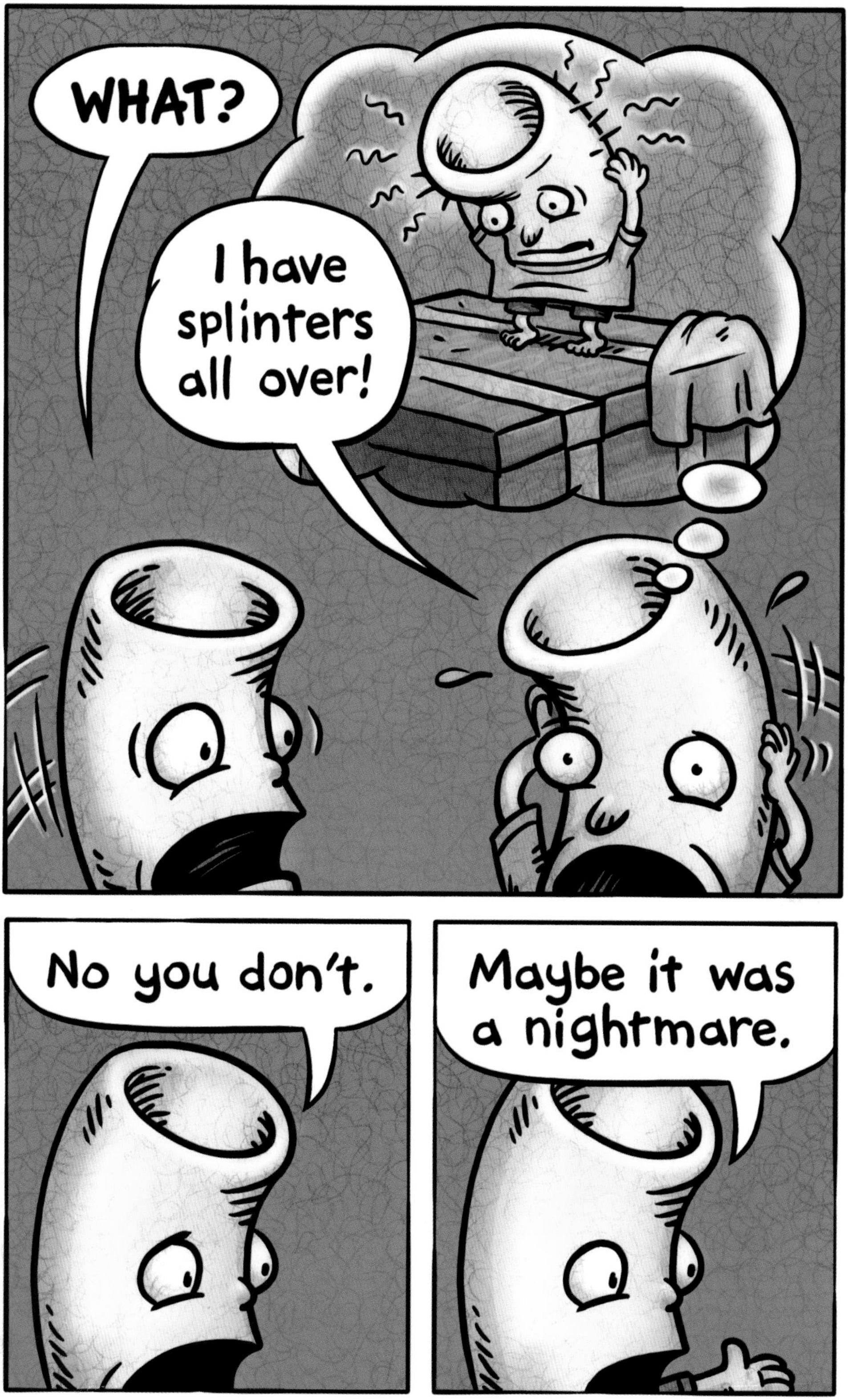
WHAT?
I have splinters all over!
No you don't.
Maybe it was a nightmare.

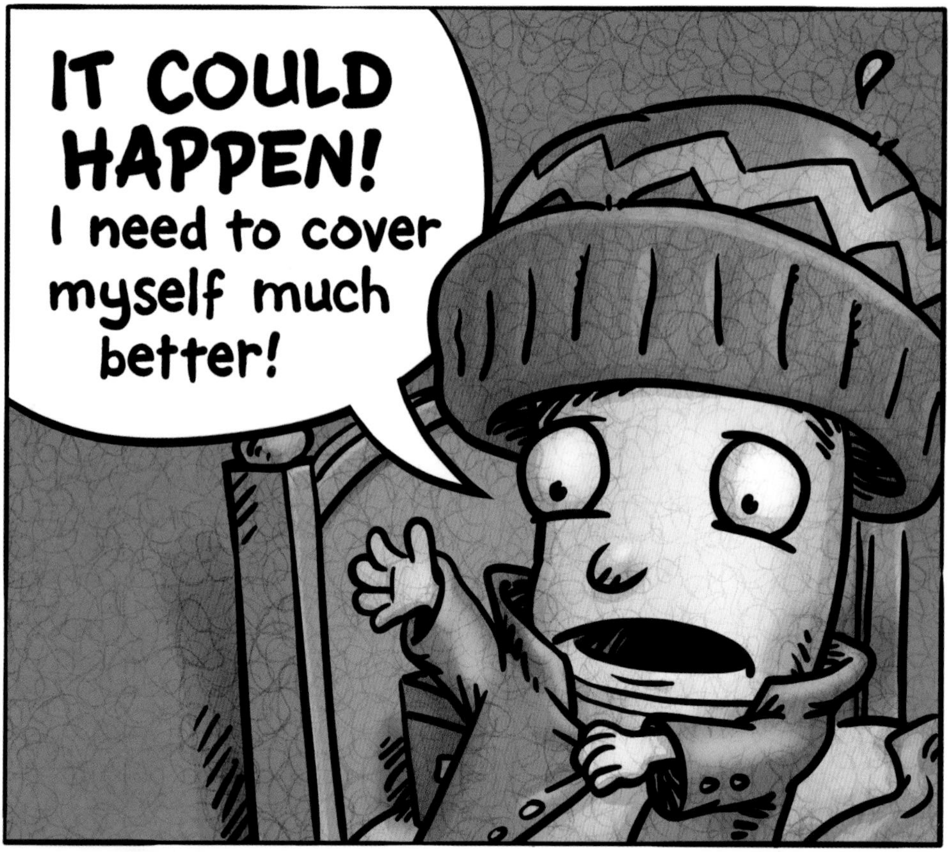
IT COULD HAPPEN! I need to cover myself much better!

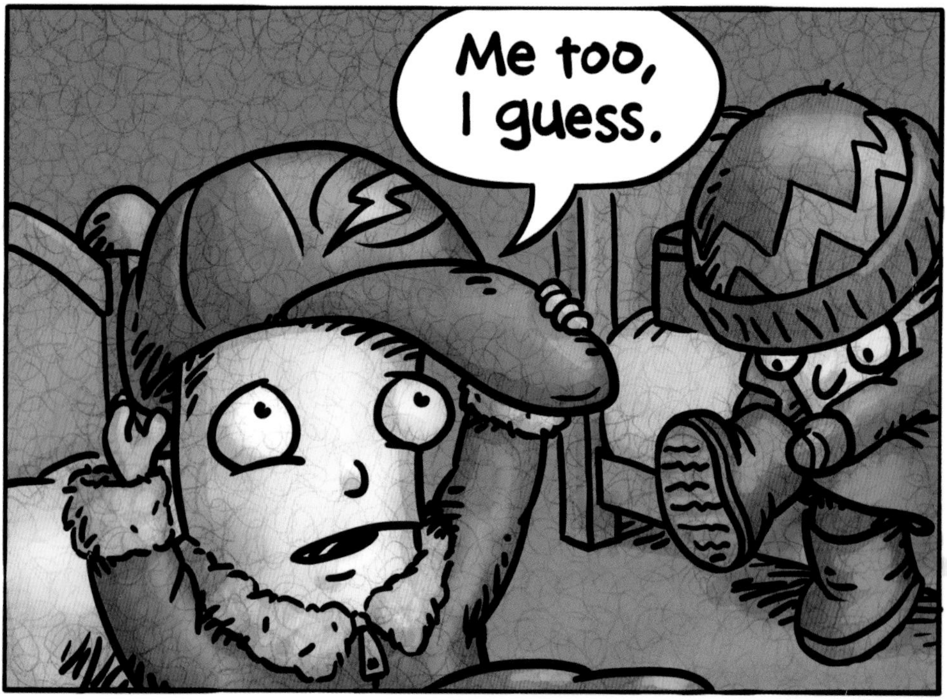
Me too, I guess.

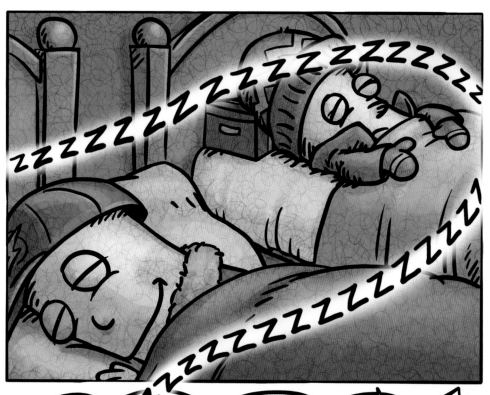

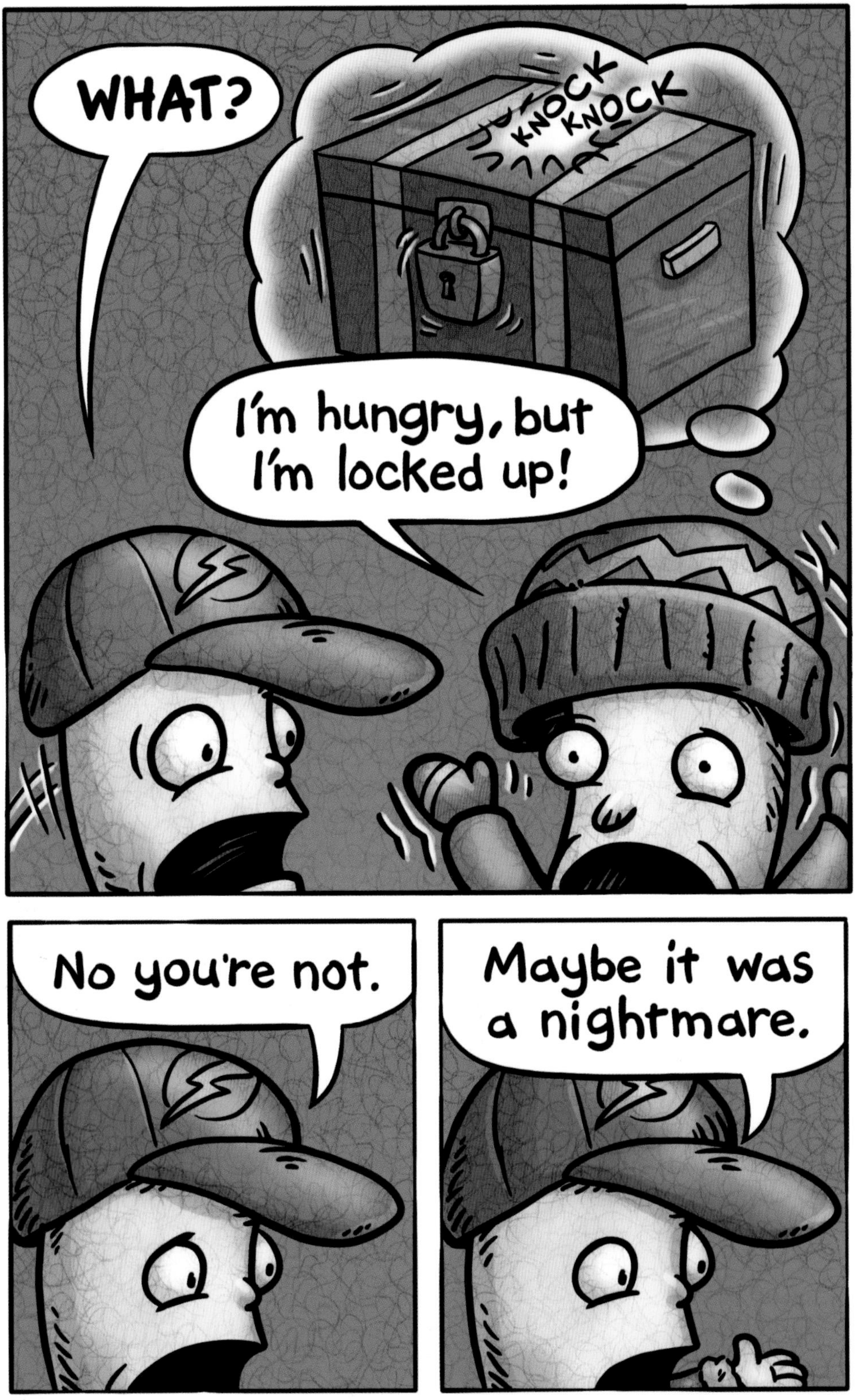
WHAT?
KNOCK
KNOCK
I'm hungry, but I'm locked up!
No you're not.
Maybe it was a nightmare.

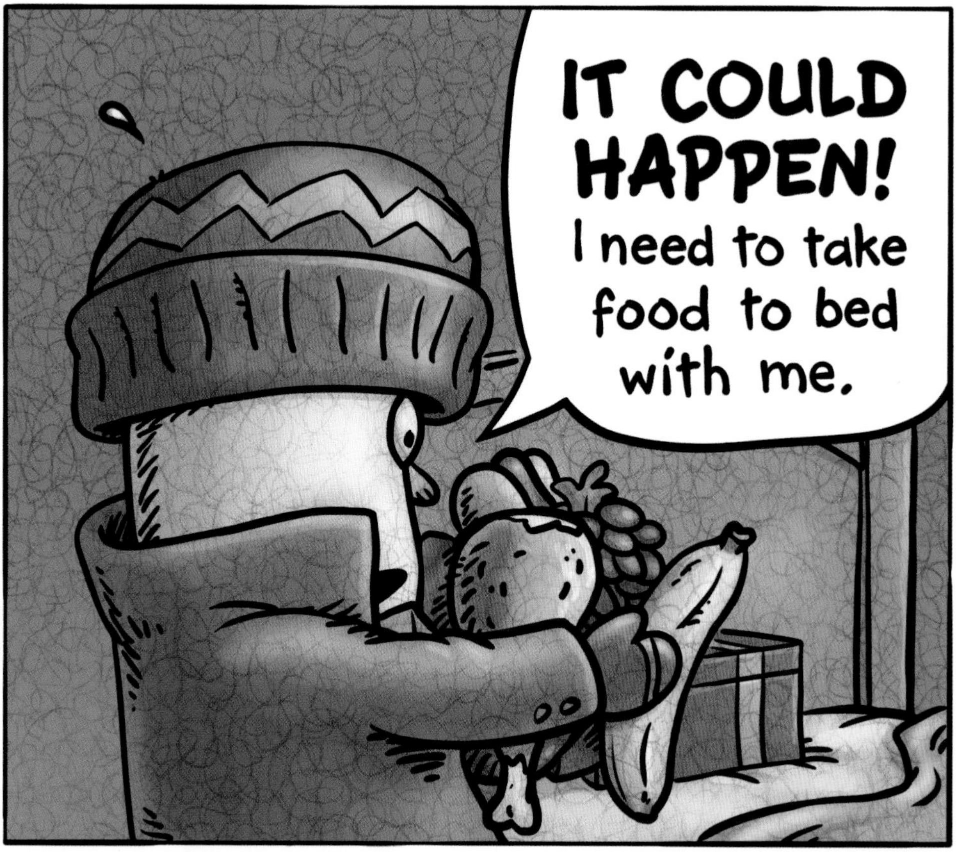
IT COULD HAPPEN! I need to take food to bed with me.

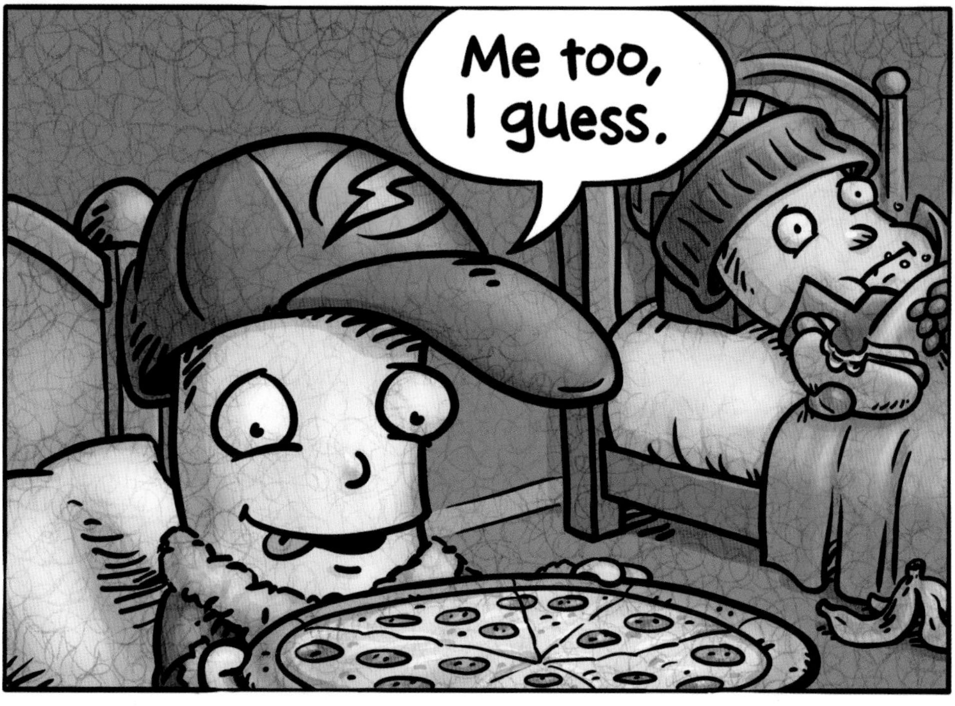
Me too, I guess.

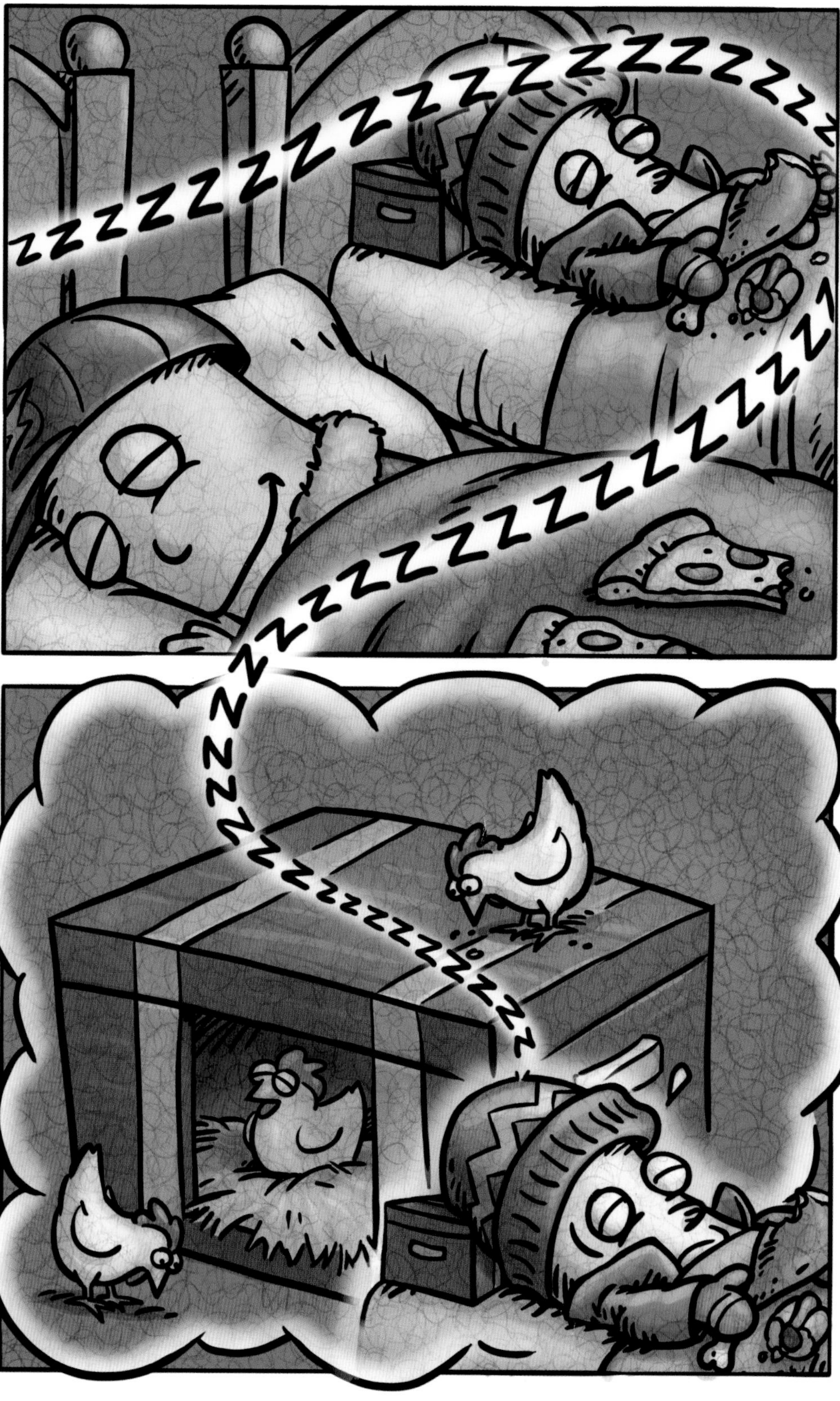

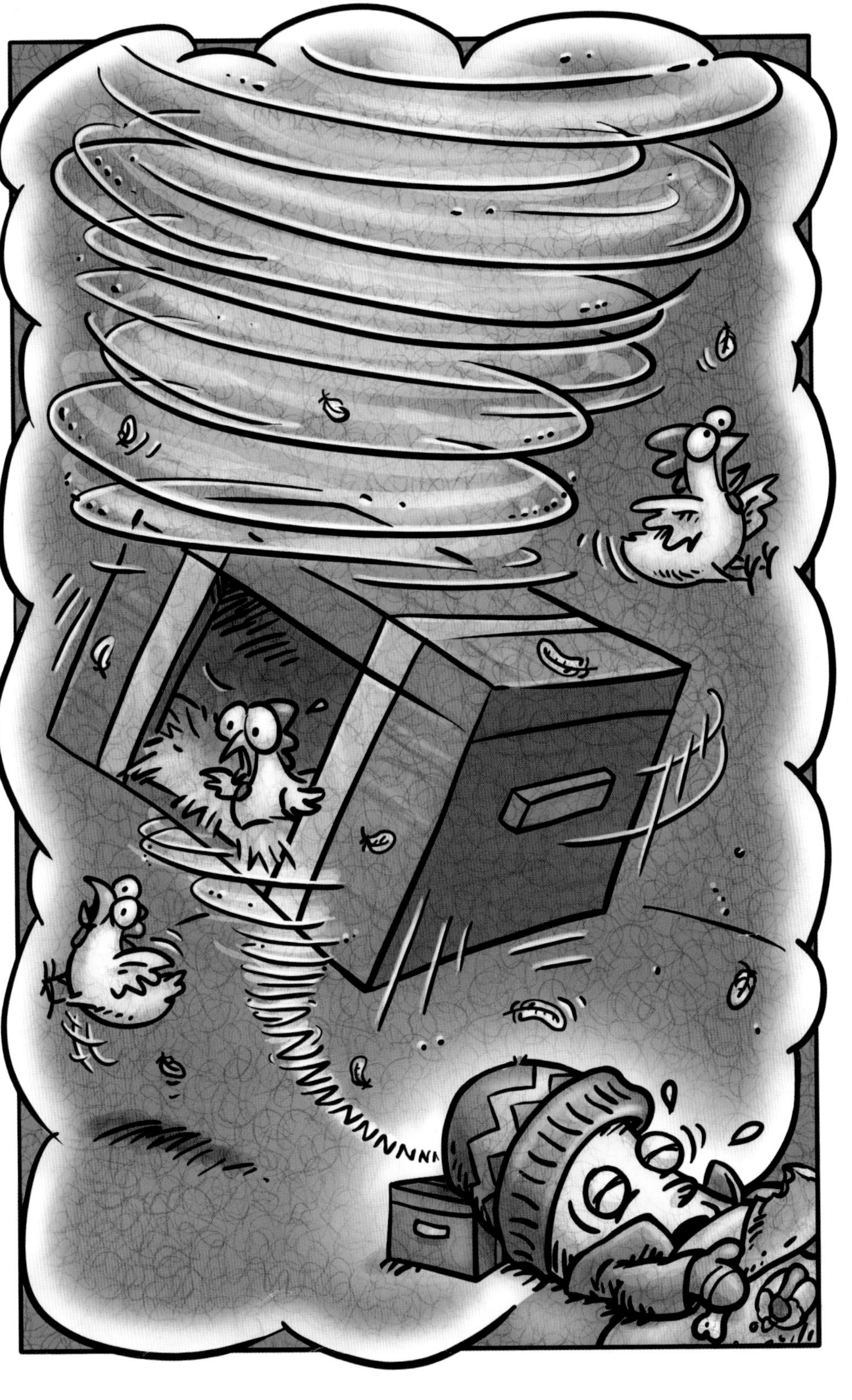

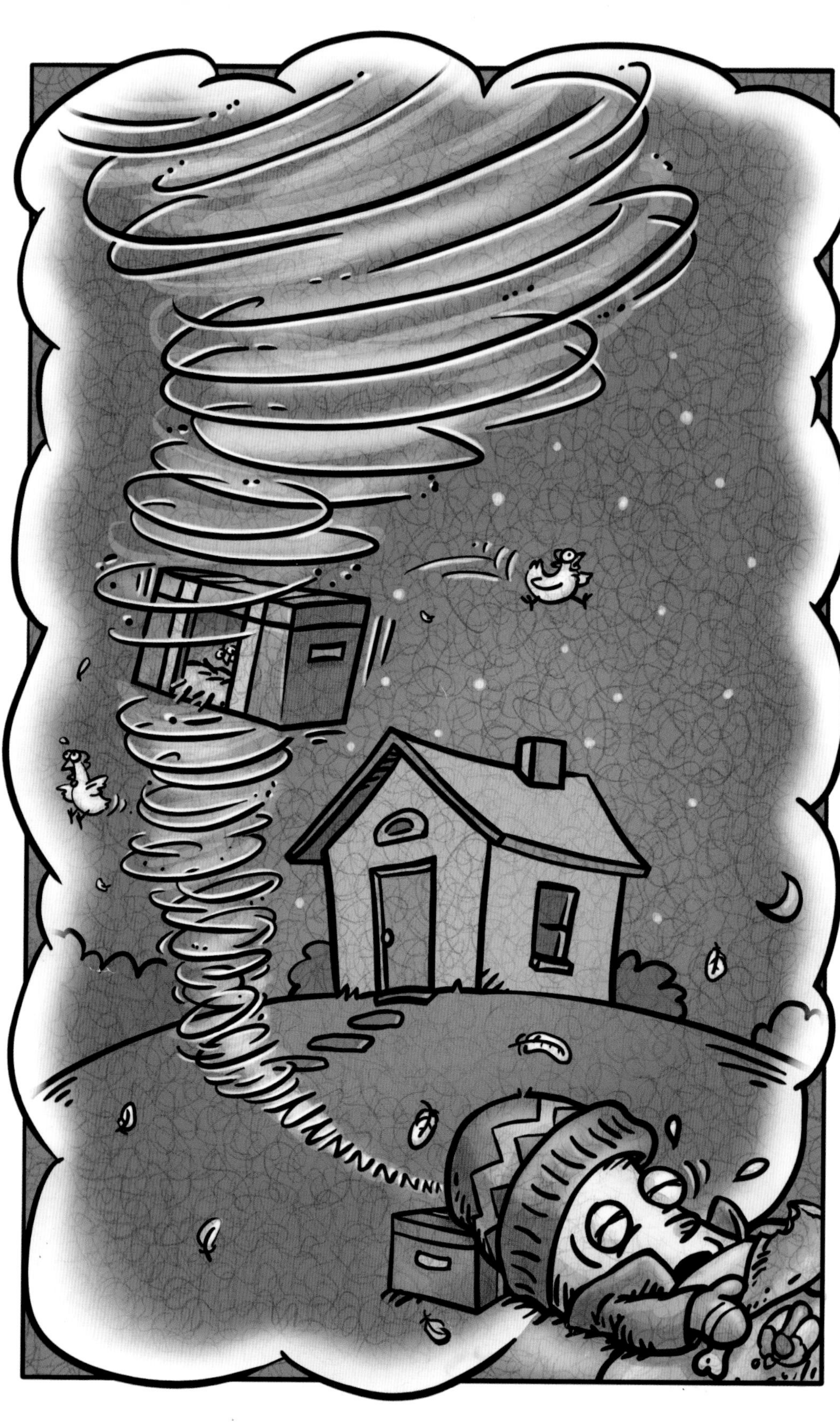

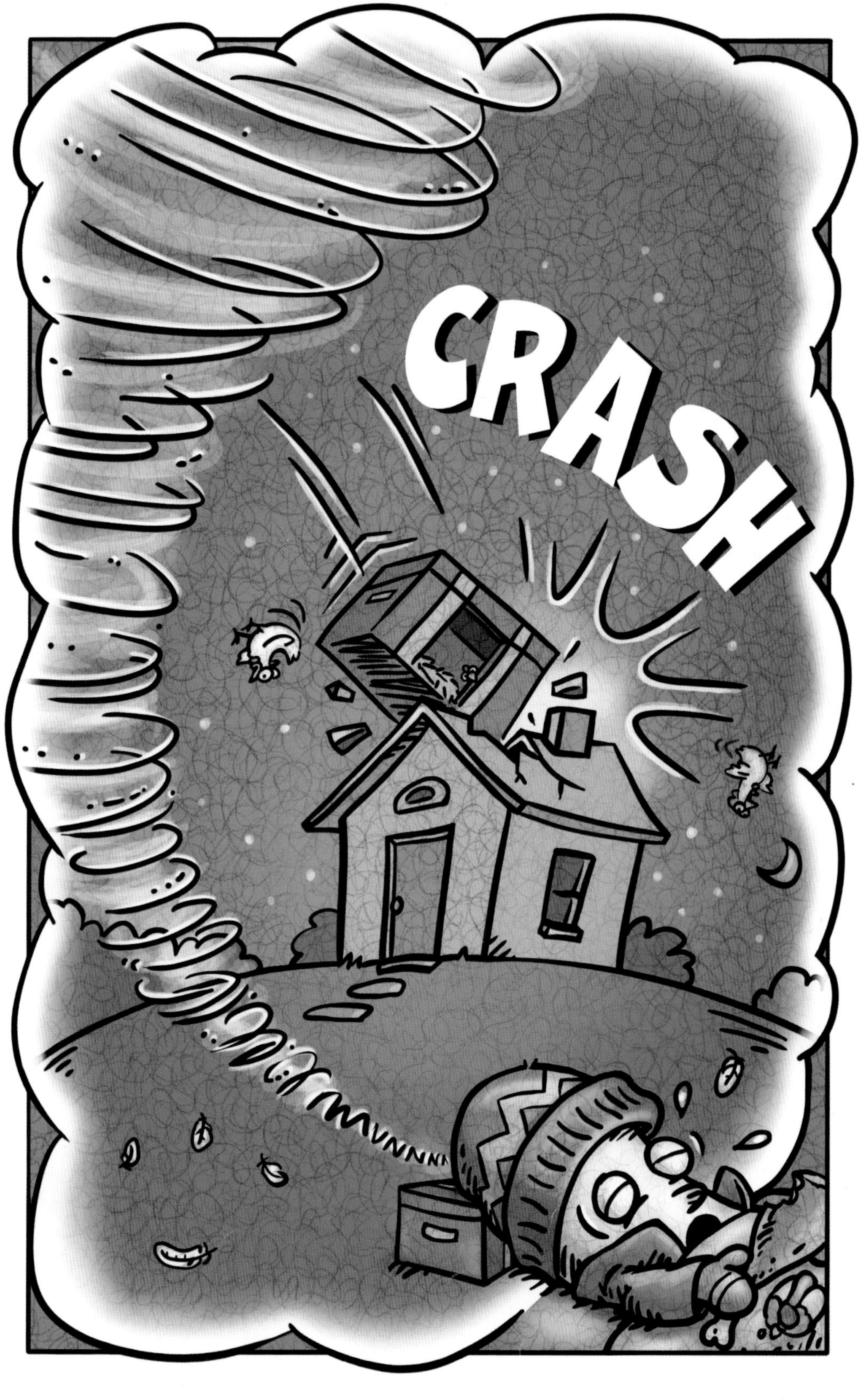
CRASH

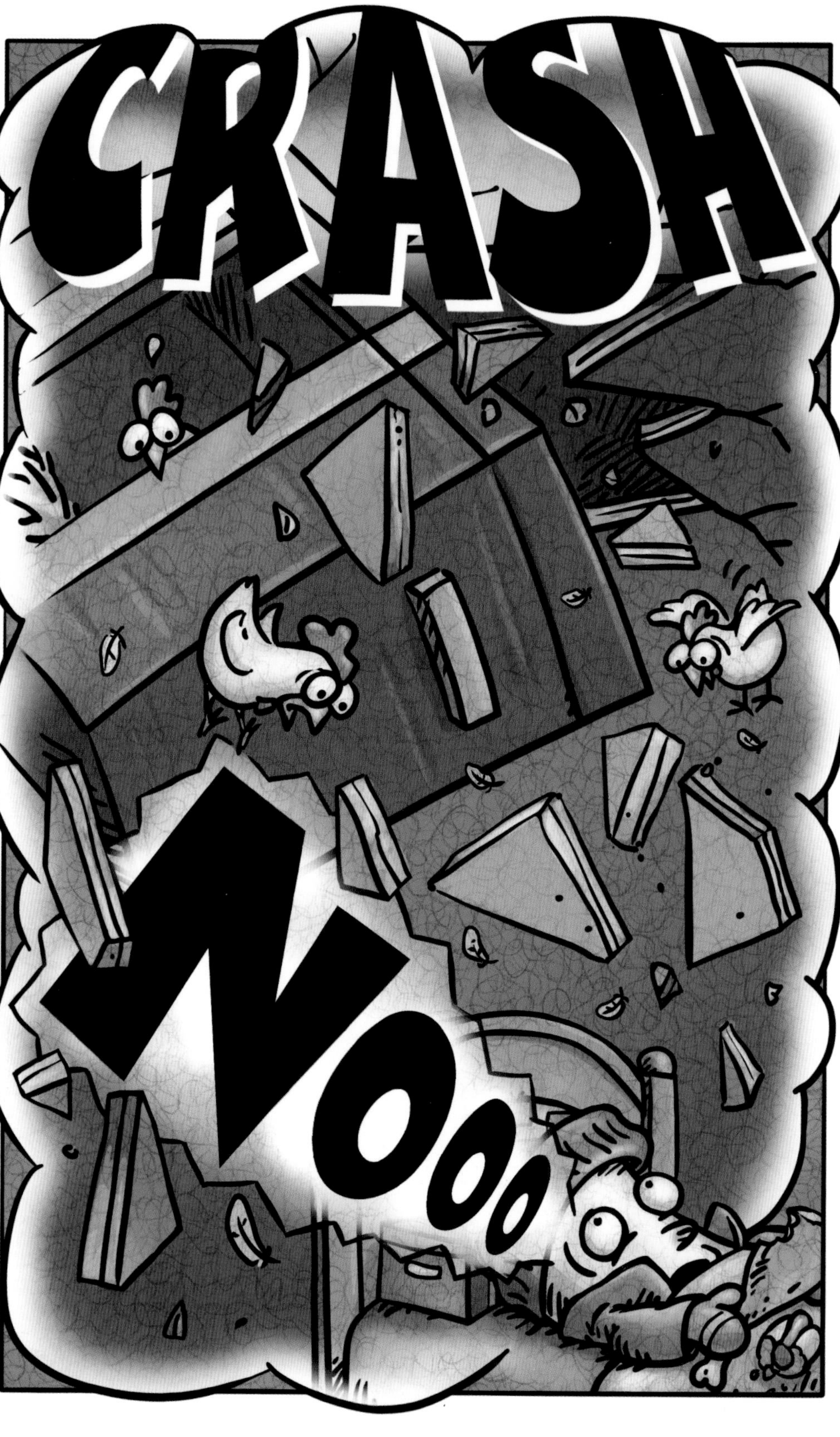
CRASH
NOooo

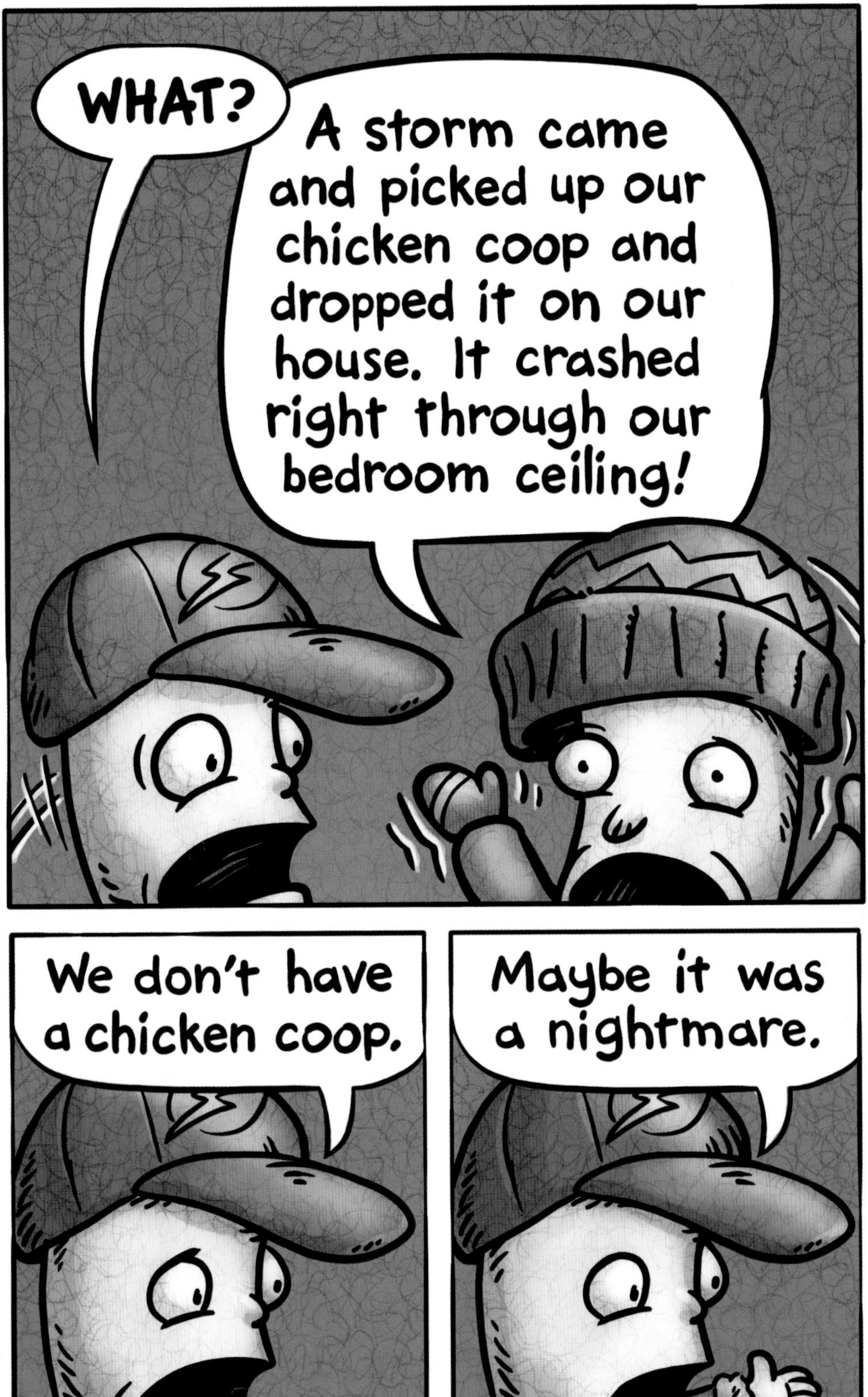
WHAT?
A storm came and picked up our chicken coop and dropped it on our house. It crashed right through our bedroom ceiling!
We don't have a chicken coop.
Maybe it was a nightmare.

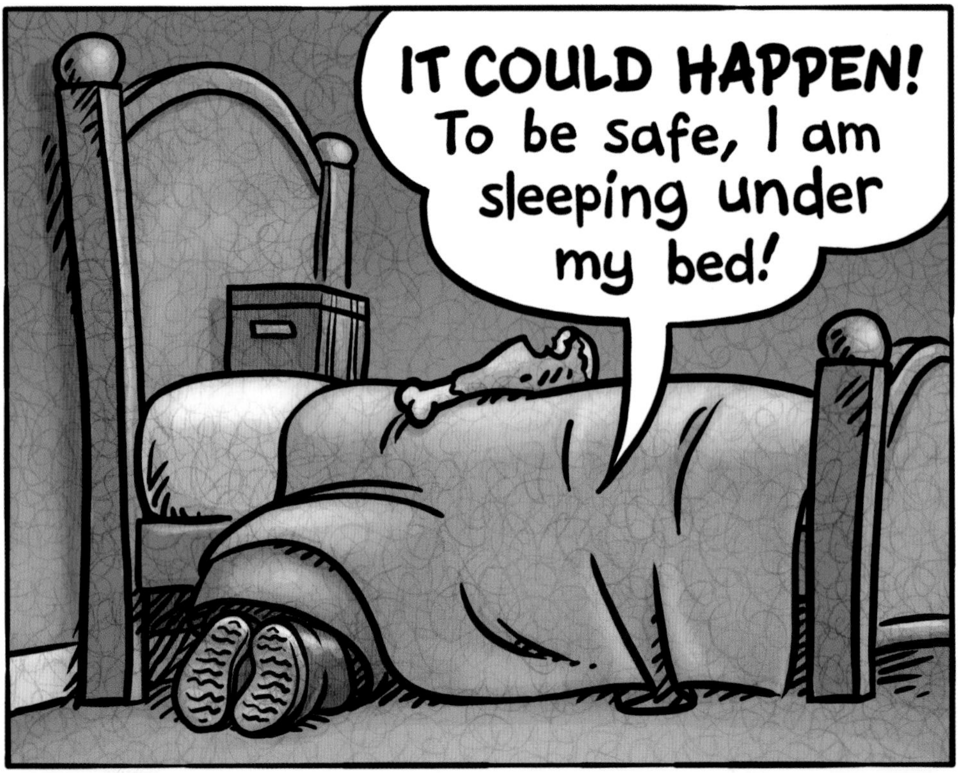
IT COULD HAPPEN! To be safe, I am sleeping under my bed!

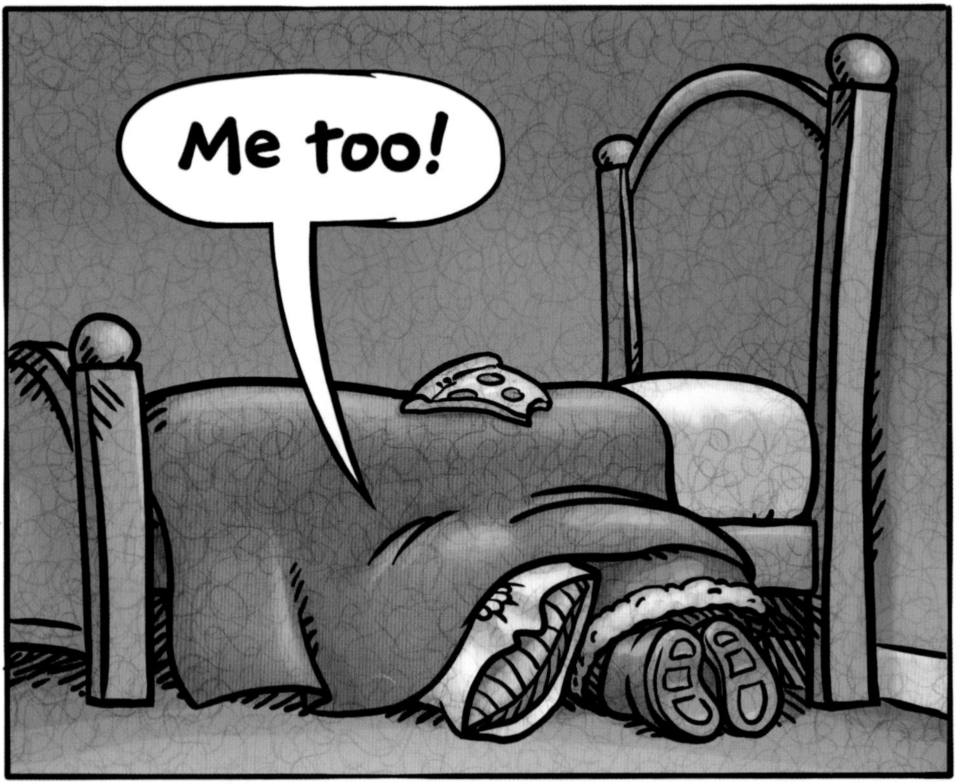
Me too!

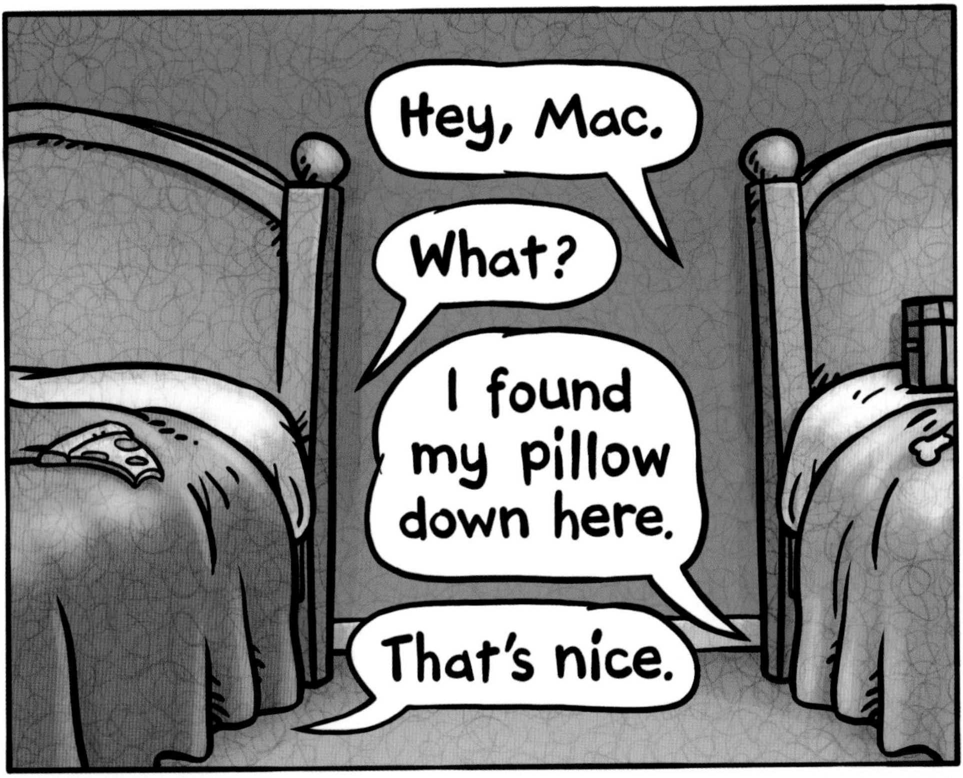
Hey, Mac.
What?
I found my pillow down here.
That's nice.

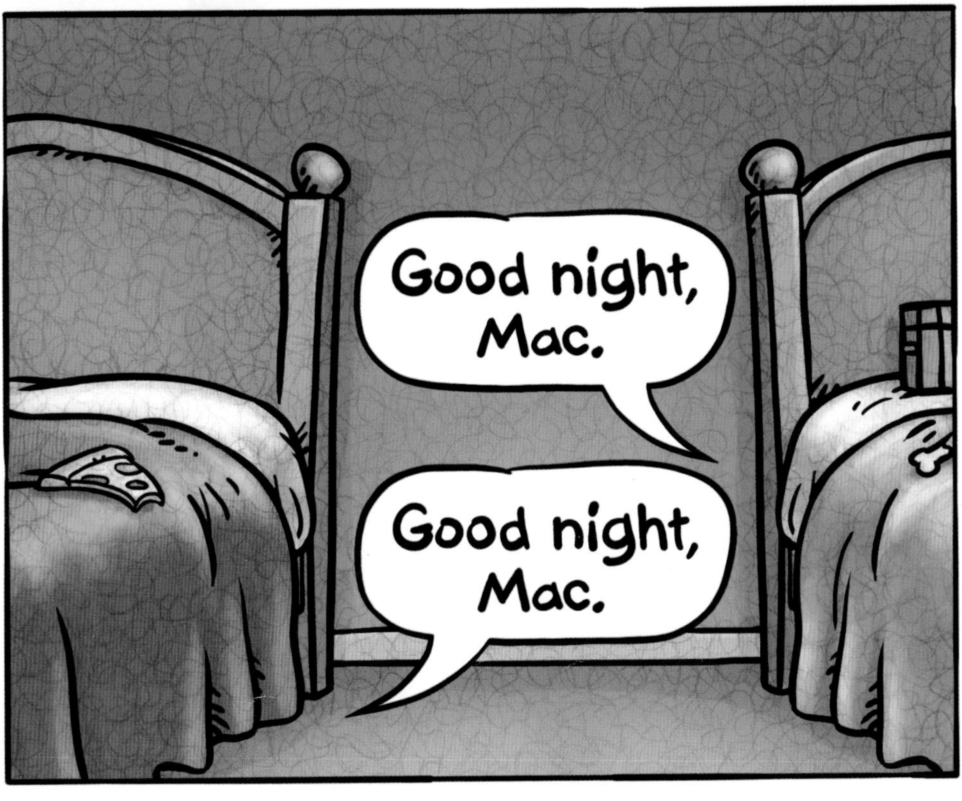
Good night, Mac.
Good night, Mac.

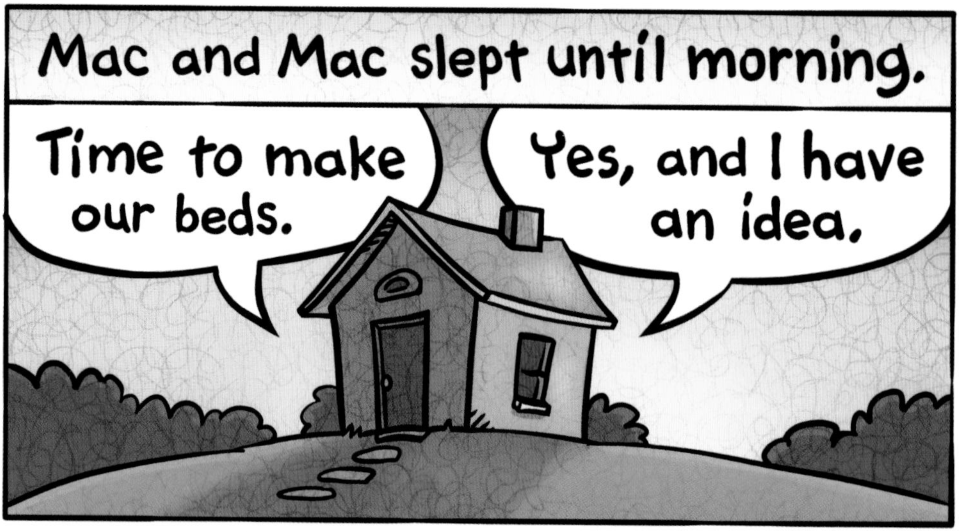
Mac and Mac slept until morning.
Time to make our beds.
Yes, and I have an idea.

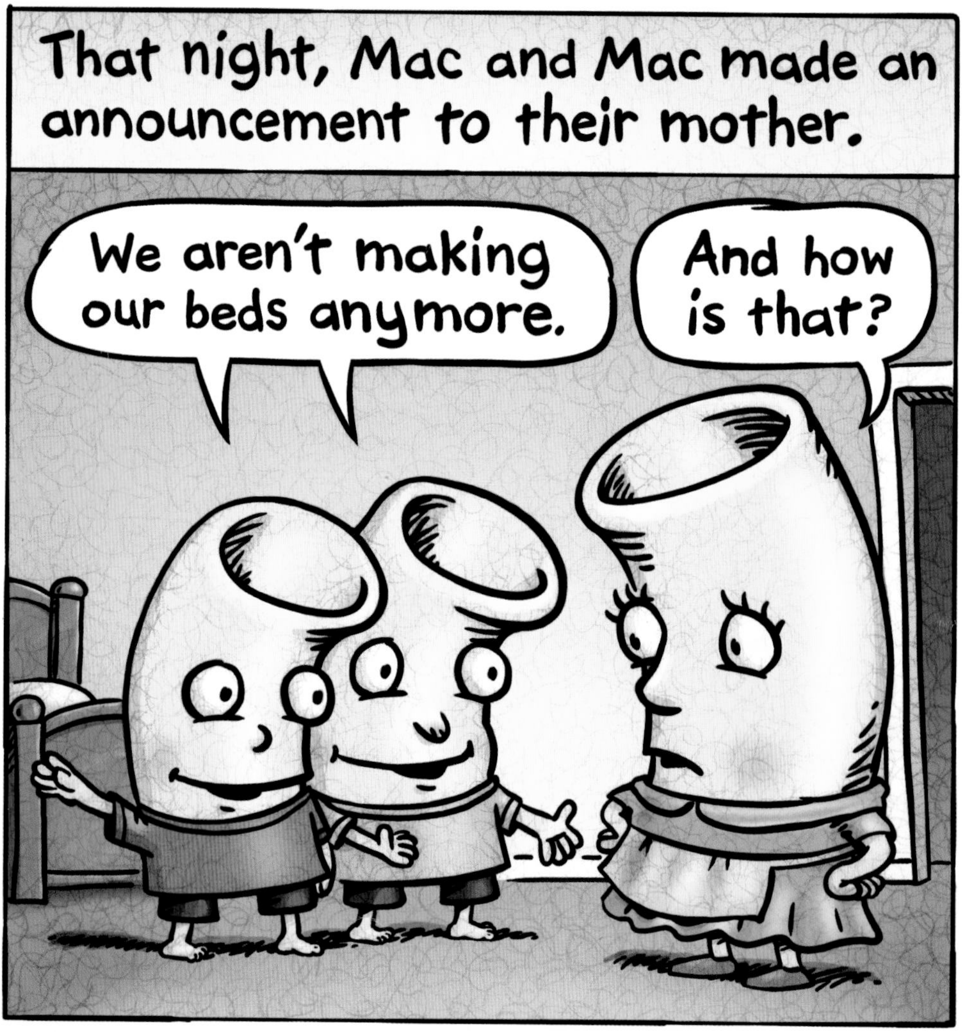
That night, Mac and Mac made an announcement to their mother.
We aren't making our beds anymore.
And how is that?

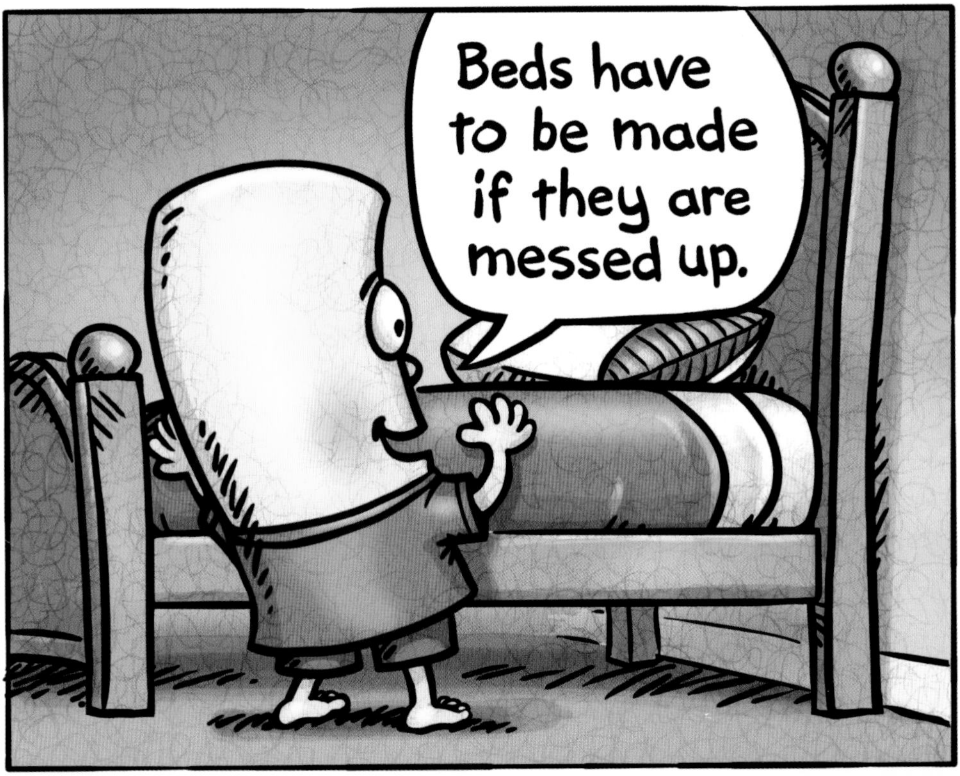
Beds have to be made if they are messed up.

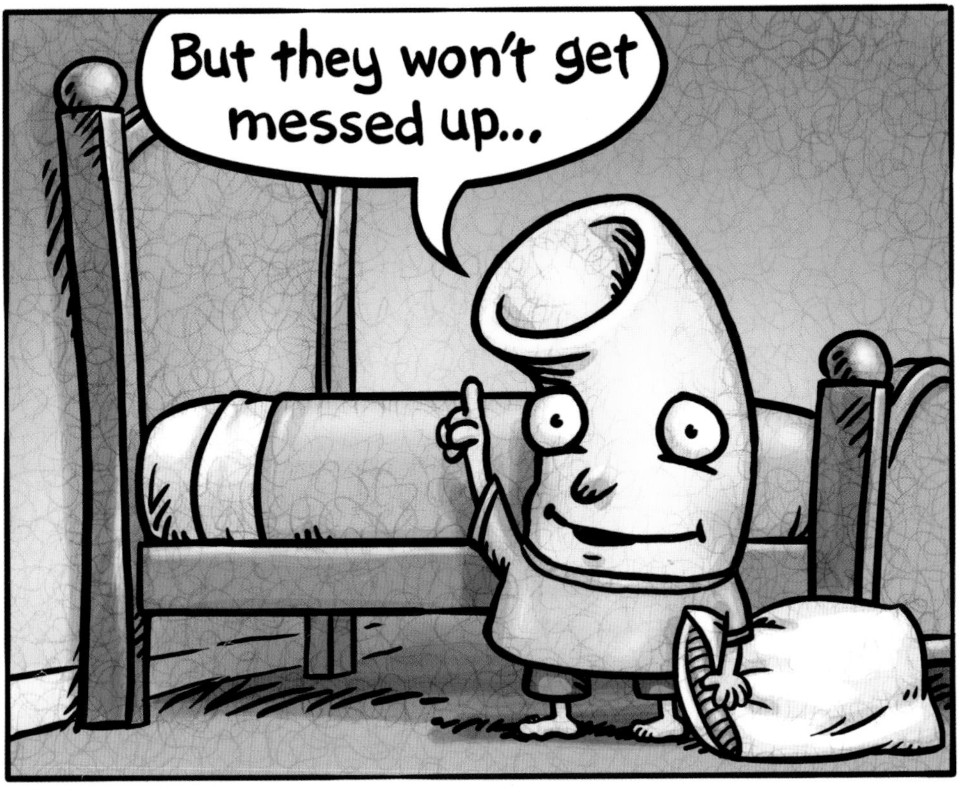
But they won't get messed up...

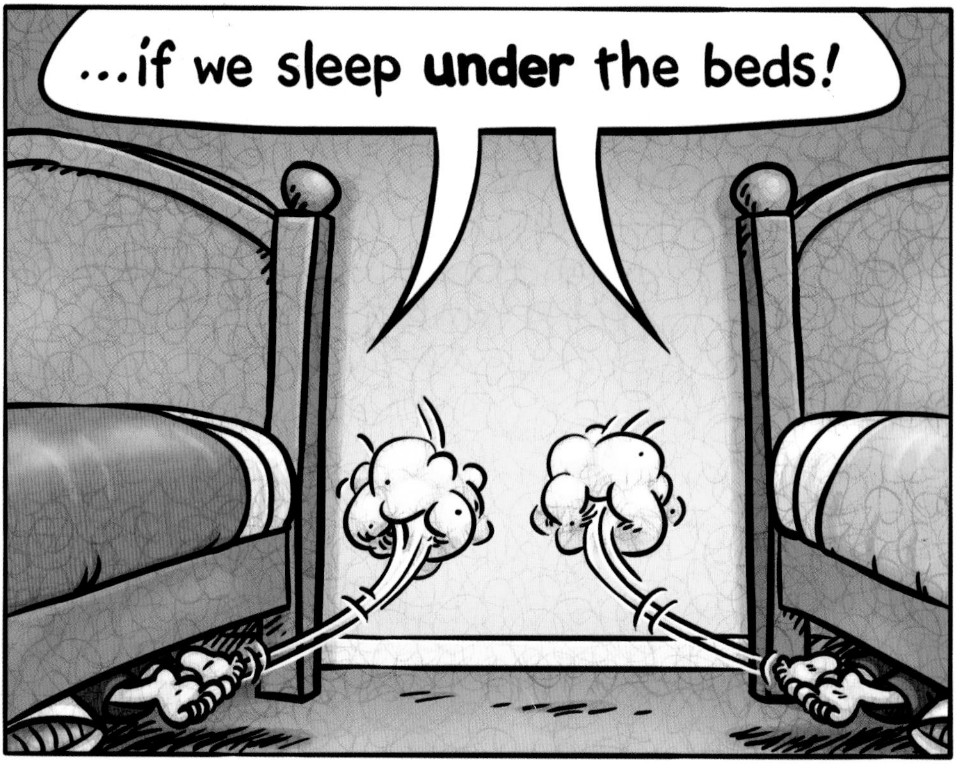
...if we sleep **under** the beds!

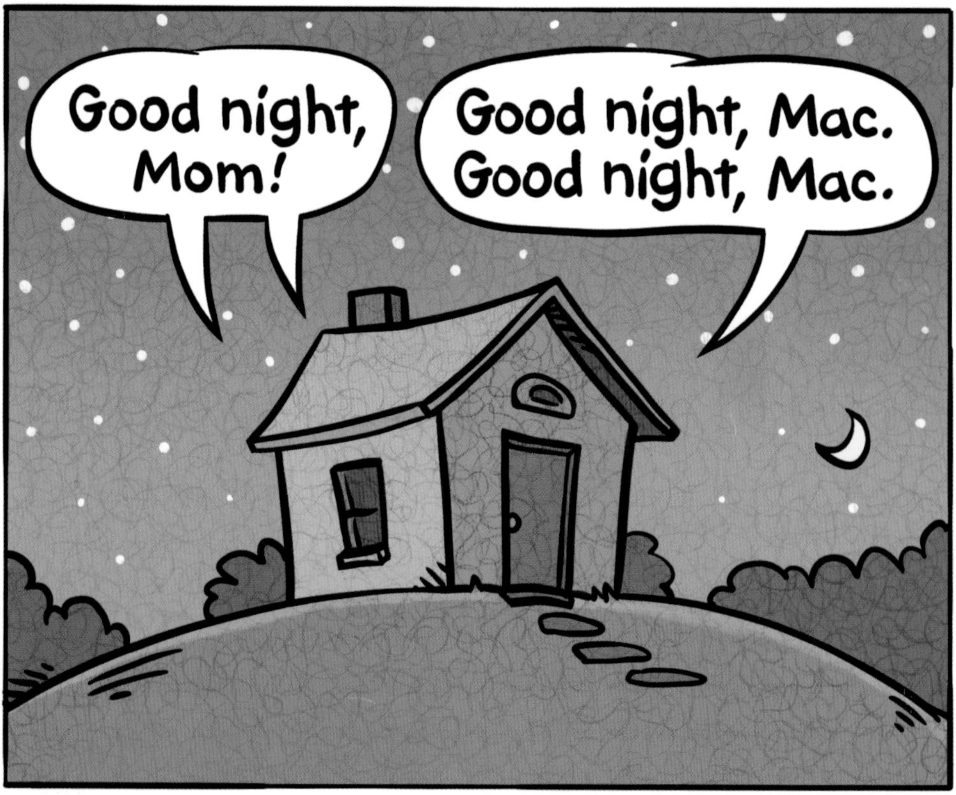
Good night, Mom!
Good night, Mac. Good night, Mac.